9/21

# UNEXPECTED
# DETOUR

*by*

*Pamela Knowles*

**Grosvenor House
Publishing Limited**

This book is published by
Grosvenor House Publishing Ltd
Link House
140 The Broadway, Tolworth, Surrey, KT6 7HT.
www.grosvenorhousepublishing.co.uk

This book is a work of fiction. Any resemblance to
people or events, past or present, is purely coincidental.

A CIP record for this book
is available from the British Library

ISBN 978-1-83975-644-3

Many thanks to Charlie,
Sharon, and Stephanie
for their support and encouragement.

# CHAPTER 1

# DEPARTURE

"Come on! Get your things together so we can go."

"I am, just give me a minute!"

"You have ten minutes young lady and then we're leaving," her father declared as he headed toward the stairs.

"Okay, I'm coming!"

It was going to be a long night! Their flight was leaving at 9:00 pm! The flight was going to take 12 hours since there weren't any direct flights from Indianapolis. They had to change planes in Toronto and then fly on to London.

Justine ran into the bathroom to make sure she had everything, especially her hairdryer. Any self-respecting fifteen-year-old, soon to be sixteen, couldn't go on any trip without the necessities, especially for three weeks! She looked around her bedroom one more time to make sure she hadn't missed anything. As soon as she was sure, she grabbed the last suitcase and hurried out the bedroom door and down the stairs. She didn't want her dad to know how excited she was about this trip so she slowed down when she got to the last step and nonchalantly entered the kitchen.

Her father, Dr. Andrew Ross, and her brother, Luke, were standing by the kitchen table. Her father had a tall, lanky build. He was always eating but never

1

seemed to put on any weight. He had a full head of hair, brown in color, and dark brown eyes. Her brother, who was two years older than she, was also thin, had dark hair, but he had their mother's bright blue eyes. Her friends at school were always commenting about his eyes and how they just loved to sit and stare at them.

When she entered the kitchen, Luke was talking to their dad about various sites he thought they ought to visit once they arrived at their destination in England. She hadn't heard the whole conversation so she wasn't sure where he wanted to go. Their dad said he would think about it and would let him know his decision when they got to London.

"I'm ready," Justine said as she strolled into the kitchen grabbing an apple.

"Well, look who's finally graced us with her presence," retorted Luke. Justine turned and opened her mouth to respond but was interrupted.

"Come on you two. Let's not start the trip with an argument. Oh, by the way, the limo won't be able to pick us up, something about engine trouble. So, we have to take my car to the airport. Grab all of your bags and put them in the SUV and be careful not to hit the sides. I don't want my brand, new SUV ruined first time out! I've already pulled it out of the garage so it will be easier to load. The bags are in the front hall. I'm going to go find your mother so we can say good-bye." With that, Dr. Ross left the two of them alone in the kitchen.

"I was trying to talk Dad into a really cool side trip when you interrupted us!" Luke stated snidely.

"I'm sorry. I was trying to hurry since Dad said he wanted to leave soon. How was I to know you were talking to Dad?"

Dr. Ross found his wife in the family room already working on some documents for the case she had been arguing in court for the past month.

2

"Oh, there you are, Stephanie," Dr. Ross said. "We're finally ready to go. I think Justine is taking everything she owns on this trip. I really wish you were going with us."

"I can't leave right now, Drew. I wish I could," Mrs. Ross looked up from her work. "But I've been thinking. It looks like this case may not take as long as I thought and I may be able to wrap it up in a day or two. And since this vacation is set for three weeks, I'll be able to come over to England and join you."

"That would be great!" Dr. Ross went over to the desk where she was seated and leaned down to give her a big hug and a kiss. "Then I hope you are able to get a swift verdict."

Justine's mom was a criminal lawyer in their home town of Indianapolis, Indiana. She was always busy defending some case in court. Her dad was a world-renowned heart surgeon. Neither one of her parents had been able to take a vacation in over two years. They were only going on this trip because her dad was speaking at a symposium in London. Justine had hoped the whole family would be going on this vacation. But her mom couldn't leave a case until it was settled so it would be just the three of them this time. She knew her dad was really looking forward to their time in England. Justine usually resented all of the time her dad spent at the hospital, but right now she was glad he was so well-known.

Justine ran into the family room slowing down once she found her parents. "Hi, Mom. I guess we're all ready to go. I'm sorry you can't come with us."

"Well, Justine, I just told your dad it looks like this case may not last much longer. So, I'll be able to join you after all."

"Wow, that's great Mom! I'm glad you'll be able to come. I don't want to be the only "girl" on the trip.

And besides, Dad doesn't really pay much attention to me, not the way you do."

"You'll be fine. Just talk to him the way you talk to me! Well, maybe not quite everything! You three have a wonderful time. Be careful! I don't want anything to happen to you. At least wait until I get there before you get into any trouble!"

"Mom, we aren't going to get into any trouble. Do we ever get into trouble here at home? Never mind, don't answer that!" Luke stated as he entered the room.

"Well, I guess we had better be going," Dr. Ross said. "We don't want to miss our plane!" And with that, all three of them kissed Mom good bye and headed out the door to their long-awaited vacation.

# CHAPTER 2

## LONG RIDE TO ENGLAND

They all climbed into the new, midnight blue SUV which was piled high with suitcases, mostly Justine's, and left for the airport. The ride to the airport took much longer than usual. It seemed like everyone had decided to go somewhere right then creating a lot of traffic. Once they arrived at the airport, they parked their car in a remote space in a Park and Ride lot since they had to leave the car at the airport while they were gone.

"Good grief, Dad! Do you think you could have parked any farther away!" Luke said sarcastically. He was somewhat disgusted that they now had to walk quite a way to catch the shuttle. "Who's going to lug all of Justine's bags to the loading area?"

"Hey, I only packed what I needed!" Justine replied.

"I don't want to return from this trip to find any dents on this expensive purchase!" their dad declared.

Luke grudgingly located a luggage cart near them and unloaded the car as fast as he could so they wouldn't miss the shuttle. Unloading the luggage was no easy task! Thank goodness, they didn't have to wait long for the shuttle and they were off to the airport. Lucky for them, the line at the check- in counter wasn't very long. They checked their luggage keeping one carry-on for the plane.

"Boy, am I glad we don't have to carry those bags anymore!" Luke said. "Why did you have to bring so much, Justine? I think you brought everything you own!" Luke wanted to assure Justine that he was not her personal valet.

"We're going to be there for three weeks! I don't know what the summer weather will be like over there. I don't know where we will be going and what I will need to wear, and what if I can't buy stuff over there to replenish what I might run out of? One has to be prepared!" Justine affirmed very matter-of-factly.

"Well, I'd say you are prepared for anything that may come your way!" Luke stated emphatically.

"Come on you two. If we don't hurry and get through security, we might miss the plane!" Dr. Ross was beginning to wish that they weren't going on this trip.

The three of them walked rather quickly to the security lines. The lines were short so they didn't have long to wait. They made it through with no glitches and walked to the gate where they would board the plane.

Within ten minutes of them arriving at the gate, the flight attendant announced that the plane would begin the boarding process. When their loading zone was called, they made their way onto the plane.

Finally, once all of the passengers had boarded, the plane left the gate. They had to wait on the tarmac for a little while since they weren't the first one in line to take off. This was Justine's favorite part of flying and she started to smirk, which was a telltale sign that she was happy. She sat back and waited for the take-off. Her brother, on the other hand, didn't like to fly and was holding the chair arms so tightly his hands were turning white. Once they had the "all clear", the big jet headed down the runway, sat back, and took off. Both of them sighed as the plane began to climb, but for different reasons. They were so excited about the trip that neither one of them could sleep on the plane. Luke and Justine each pulled out a travel guide to read about England.

"Look, here's a page on Stonehenge! That's one of the places I was talking to Dad about. It's definitely a place I want to see. I think we need to go there! Here, you can read about it." Luke handed the travel guide to Justine. This seemed to Justine like it would be one of the most intriguing sights to see while they were in England. They read everything they could about it and both decided that it was one place they didn't want to miss.

They finally landed in London after a two-hour delay in Toronto. As soon as they stepped foot in the airport, both Luke and Justine had trouble containing their excitement. Justine kept making screaming noises and Luke kept mumbling, "I can't believe we're really here!" After a "high five" to each other, the family went to pick up their luggage.

On the way, a store display caught Justine's attention and she grabbed her brother's arm and pulled him backwards. "Luke, take a look at that! London knows we're here!"

There in front of them was a copy of the London Times with a picture of their dad on the front page. The headline read, "World-Renowned Heart Surgeon Comes to London".

Dr. Ross stopped when he saw that the kids weren't next to him. He turned around to see where they were and noticed they had stopped and were staring at something. "What are you two staring at?"

"Dad, there's a picture of you in the paper!" Luke was pointing at the newsstand.

"Where?" and he picked up a paper. "Oh, wow, I'm on the front page! Well, a reporter called the day before we left home and had a lot of questions about me, the symposium, and my speech. I didn't realize it would make the front page!" Dr. Ross was clearly surprised to see himself in one of London's top newspapers.

"Wow, Dad! I knew you were important back home, but not that important! I'm impressed!" Justine stated as she began to realize how good a doctor her father really was.

"I was asked to give a speech, that's all," her dad answered very humbly.

"Just a speech?" Luke replied as he picked up the paper in astonishment. "It says here that you are the foremost heart surgeon in the world, Dad! That's huge! Man, I had no idea you were that good!"

Justine and Luke now looked at their father with a new awareness and awe knowing what he had accomplished. They bought a newspaper as a souvenir and continued on their way to retrieve their luggage.

# CHAPTER 3

## THEIR ARRIVAL

As they exited the luggage area, they noticed a man holding a sign that read, 'Dr. Ross'. "I'm Dr. Ross," he said as they approached the man.

"Glad to meet you, sir. I'm here to take you to the hotel. The car is just outside that door over there. Here, let me help you with your luggage."

They all walked outside and waiting for them was a shiny black limousine. Justine and Luke gave each other a high five and climbed into the limo. Once they were inside, Justine noticed a present on the seat that had her name on it.

"I wonder where this came from?"

"Well, read the card," Luke encouraged.

"Okay. It says, 'A gift for you'. Do you suppose it's an early birthday present?"

"I don't know. Open it and let's see what's inside."

She couldn't stand not knowing what was in the box. Her curiosity got the best of her so she unwrapped the box and carefully opened it. She slowly pulled the tissue off the top and found hiding underneath a beautiful necklace with a colorful pendant attached. She couldn't quite make out the intricate design on the pendant but thought it looked like something she might find in an antique store.

"This is beautiful!"

"Try it on."

She figured no one would care if she just tried it on. She undid the clasp and placed it around her neck. She looked around the limo to find a mirror but couldn't find one.

"How do I look?" Justine asked.

"That really looks great!" Luke said as he admired her new gift.

After her dad had gotten in the limo, Justine immediately hugged him.

"Well, that was a surprise," her dad said. "Where did that come from?"

"I want to thank you and mom for this beautiful necklace. I'm supposing it's an early birthday present."

"That is beautiful," her dad said as he reached over to examine it. "But that present didn't come from us. Maybe this is from the committee who put together the symposium."

"Hey, if that's the case, why didn't I get something, too?" Luke threw in.

"Well, I don't care where it came from. I'm definitely going to keep it no matter who gave it to me."

"I would recommend that you wear it under your shirt. It may be worth something and I don't want you to be in any danger while you wear it," her dad informed her.

The weather was glorious despite all they had heard about how London was usually rainy. The limo driver stated that the director of the symposium had arranged for the family to stay at The Ritz London.

On the way, Luke "googled" the Ritz on his phone and read the ad for the hotel. "'Overlooking Green Park, it has opulent, luxurious bedrooms, period architecture, antique furnishings, high ceilings, ornate fireplaces, chandeliers, and a terrace. It serves afternoon tea. It is centrally located near Buckingham Palace, the

Tower of London, Big Ben, and Piccadilly Circus.' Wow, this place sounds awesome! I can't believe we're staying there!"

The limo pulled up in front of a beautiful, very tall, older hotel in London. They were greeted by the hotel doorman. He opened the limo door and stated in very proper English, "Welcome to London, Dr. Ross. We have been expecting you. I will take care of the luggage for you." As they started into the hotel, they could hear the doorman and the limo driver talking about something as they stood near the trunk of the limo.

Luke poked his sister, "I bet they're talking about the number of bags he has to unload." He wasn't going to let her forget about all the work she had caused for him so far on this trip.

As Luke and Justine walked into the lobby, their eyes opened in amazement. Everywhere they looked they saw statues and architecture so much older than anything in the United States. It was so awesome to be standing in the same place as many of the important people they had read about in school. Even their dad was standing there wide-eyed as he gazed at their surroundings.

As Justine was looking at the various architectural markings in the lobby, she noticed a tall figure dressed all in black staring at them. She couldn't tell if it was a man or a woman since the figure was draped in a floor length cape and had a large hood covering its face. The figure was standing in the shadow of one of the large columns which lined the lobby. She immediately turned back around, tugged at her dad's jacket and asked, "Hey, Dad, do you see that person over there?" As she turned back around to point out the position of the figure, it was gone.

"What, what did you say, Justine?" Dad asked.

"Oh, nothing. I guess I was just seeing things." She decided her mind must have been playing tricks on her and she just chalked it up to being very tired from the plane ride.

They walked up to the front desk to check in and before Dr. Ross opened his mouth the desk clerk acknowledged them. "Greetings, Dr. Ross. We're so happy you'll be staying with us during your visit in London," the desk clerk stated as he handed Dr. Ross the keys to their room. "You have a suite on the twelfth floor."

"I was just wondering," Dr. Ross inquired, "How did you know who I was?"

"Your picture is in the paper and all over the news on the Telly," the clerk replied.

"Oh, okay, thank you." Dr. Ross was somewhat baffled by all of the press his visit was getting.

As they approached the elevator, Luke looked at Justine and stated, "Pip, pip, tally ho and all that!" They both laughed at his attempt at an English accent and got on the elevator. When they had reached the twelfth floor, the doors of the elevator opened, they stepped off, and began searching for their room number. Having finally found it, they opened the door to their room and everything Luke had read about the rooms was true! The room was spectacular! They were greeted by two large windows on the far side of the room. They couldn't wait to see the view and immediately ran to the windows and walked out on the terrace. The view of the city was amazing! They could even see Buckingham Palace in the distance.

"Hey, Dad, can we go to Buckingham Palace to see the changing of the guard?" Justine inquired in an eager voice.

"Yes, we'll go there, but not right now."

"Well, I kinda knew it wouldn't be right now. What time is it anyway?"

"Because of the time difference, and that unexpected delay, it is 6:00 in the evening. So, we won't be able to see that or anything else until tomorrow. Right now, I suggest we find somewhere to eat. I don't know about you two, but I'm starving!"

"Wow, I totally forgot about the time difference! I was still going by my own watch! Now that you mention it, I'm famished," Justine said. "Let's find somewhere to eat! After we eat, I guess we will need to come back here and go to bed! This time difference is going to take some getting used to!"

"I could go for a good hamburger right now," Luke threw in.

But before they left the room, Justine had to stop in front of the mirror. She stood there looking at herself, admiring the pendent around her neck. The links were small and dainty but it didn't seem as if it could break. And the pendant was oval in shape with many bright iridescent colors crisscrossing it. As she stood there, it began to glow sending streams of light out from the oval. It startled her and she immediately took it off. Once it was off, the light vanished. She examined the pendant looking to see if it had a button that would activate the light, but she couldn't find anything. So, if there wasn't anything to turn it on, then how did it all of a sudden light up. She decided to put it back on and immediately tucked it back in her shirt.

"Dad, this necklace just lit up and I don't know how it happened! Dad? Luke? Where are you?"

She realized they had already gone out the door and were waiting for her in the hallway.

"Did you hear what I said?" she asked after she joined them.

"No, I'm sorry, Justine. Luke and I were talking and walked out into the hallway thinking you were right behind us."

"Well, I wasn't! I was standing in front of the mirror looking at my necklace, and it all of a sudden lit up! I couldn't find anything that would make it do that. How could that happen?"

"I don't know. There must be a trigger of some sort that would make it do that. You just don't see it. Don't worry about it. Let's just get something to eat right now, okay?"

"Okay, Dad. But I'm telling you right now, it was strange!"

The three of them stopped in the lobby to ask about restaurants in the area. The concierge said there was a little hamburger place around the corner so they decided to eat there.

When they arrived at the restaurant, Dr. Ross asked if they could sit by a window so they could enjoy the London street. The menu included many traditional dishes and also the good ole hamburger, which both of the teens ordered. After they had eaten, Luke said, "I actually liked the hamburger! It was a lot better than anything I've had at home!"

"Me, too." Justine added as she finished her last bite. She looked across the table at Luke and burped.

"Oh wow, Justine! Don't you have any better manners than that?" Luke stated as he pretended to be disgusted by her lack of manners.

As Justine turned to look out the window, she saw the same figure, or at least she thought it was the same one, standing across the street. It seemed to be watching them intently as they finished their meal. "Who wears clothes like that anymore?" she thought to herself.

"Dad, I don't want to alarm anyone, but I think someone is following us".

"How could anyone be following us? No one knows us over here." Luke questioned. "I retract that statement. I forgot Dad's face is plastered all over the place!"

"Justine, no one is following us, honey. I think you are just seeing things," her dad kindly replied.

"No, I saw someone standing across the street watching us! I'm serious! It had a long black cape on and a hood over its head just like the one I saw in the hotel!" And as she looked across the street, the area where she thought she had seen someone was empty, just bare sidewalk. Now she was almost convinced that the long trip must be playing tricks in her mind. She must be more tired than she thought!

"You've been reading too many mysteries," Luke said.

"Well, I guess we had better get back to the hotel since it's now 8:30 here. I'm not tired anymore, but I certainly don't want to stay up all night."

And with that, Justine picked up her purse and slid out of the booth. As they walked back to the hotel, she couldn't shake the feeling that someone was always following them and she kept looking back over her shoulder to see if anyone was there. She was very glad to finally arrive back at their hotel room because she knew whatever was stalking them wouldn't be there, at least she hoped it wouldn't.

Before she got into bed, she took the necklace off and laid it on the bedside table. She sat on the edge of the bed for a while just staring at it. Where did it come from, who gave it to her and why? She decided she wasn't going to know the answers to those questions at least not right now, so she should just enjoy the gift despite her reservations about it. She let out a big yawn, lay down in the bed, pulled the covers over her and drifted off to sleep.

# CHAPTER 4

## FIRST LIGHT/FIRST DAY

The next morning, the sun filled the room with light waking Dr. Ross bright and early.

"Up and at 'em you two!" Dad said as he stood between the two bedrooms.

"I can't believe it's time to get up! I'm still tired! I couldn't get to sleep last night," moaned Justine from the bed in her room.

"Come on you two! This is our first day in London," Dr. Ross said excitedly. "We need to get some breakfast and be on our merry way, as the British might say. How do you like that, now I'm a poet!"

"Dad, do you have to be so cheerful?" Luke said as he pulled the pillow over his head.

"Yes, I do! This is my, our vacation. I have one week before the symposium starts and I don't want to waste a minute of it!"

"Okay, okay. I'm getting out of bed," Justine replied as she slowly moved her body to the edge of the bed, sat up, and opened her eyes. The sunlight greeted her like twinkling diamonds in the room. She sat staring as the morning seemed to unfold right before her eyes.

Now that she was awake, her brother needed to be awake, too. She picked up her pillow, walked silently over to his bed, and socked him in the head.

"Ow-w-w-w!!" yelled Luke. "That hurt! What's wrong with you?"

"Nothing. I just thought you ought to be awake!" Justine replied.

"Okay, now that everyone is awake, hurry up and get dressed so we can start sightseeing," Dr. Ross said as he pulled on his shorts. "Where do we go today? Anyone have any suggestions?"

"Let's begin in London and when Mom gets here, we can go visit places outside of London," Justine stated with conviction.

"Great idea," Dr. Ross affirmed.

"Looks like I don't get to vote. London it is," Luke acquiesced as he got out of bed.

Justine got dressed and put on the necklace. She wasn't going to leave something that beautiful just lying around. She noticed that it glistened in the sunlight. As she continued to stare at it, there was a small flash of light in the center of it and then it was gone. "There it is again! But this time it wasn't as bright! I must be seeing things," she said quietly to herself.

"Dressed already? I thought we would be waiting at least an hour for you to get ready," her dad quipped.

"Nope. We don't get to tour London every day!"

"I see you're wearing your necklace. It's very pretty."

"Look at the design on the pendant, Dad. Does it look like anything familiar?"

"I've never seen anything like it. It looks like it might be an antique."

"That's what I thought, too."

"Can I wear it today when we go sightseeing?" Justine looked at her dad with her big eyes and cocked her head because she knew when she did, he would always say yes.

"I suppose you can wear it today. What else am I going to say. You already have it on!"

"Thanks, Dad! You're the greatest!"

"Yah, I know. Just don't lose it!"

"I promise I'll take good care of it!" She decided to tuck it inside her tee shirt so nothing would happen to it. She might bring it out if she wanted to impress anyone during the day.

"I'm glad you like the necklace, Justine."

"What? Dad, did you say something?"

"What? I just asked you to be careful not to lose the necklace."

"No, after that."

"Don't think I said anything else."

"Hmmm, I could have sworn I heard you say something...only it really didn't sound like your voice."

"Luke, are you dressed yet? I really would like to get our day started."

"Yes, Dad, I was ready before Justine."

"Great! Get any last-minute items and let's go."

The weather that day was supposed to be hot, and Luke and Justine were wearing shorts. They grabbed their guide books about England, the camera, the key and headed out the door. After locking the door, they walked to the elevator. Luke pushed the down button and they waited for the elevator to arrive which didn't take very long.

They got on the elevator and turned around to face the front. That's when Justine saw the figure, dressed in black, standing in the hallway facing them. As the elevator door was closing, her gaze followed it until the door closed and she couldn't see the figure anymore. She straightened back up and her mind flashed back to last night when they were sitting in the restaurant. This made the third time she had seen the figure in black and now she knew her mind couldn't be playing tricks on her as she had originally thought. The elevator reached the ground floor and the door opened.

"Dad, did you see a person standing in the hallway when we got on the elevator?" Justine could hardly get the words out as she stepped off the elevator.

"What?" her dad asked as he turned toward her. He saw the look of –horror-- on her face and became worried. "Justine, are you alright? You look rather pale."

"Did either one of you see the person who was standing in the hallway when we got on the elevator?" She asked as she started to panic.

"What person? The hallway was clear," her dad stated "Luke, did you see anyone?"

"No. The hallway was totally empty when we got on. There wasn't anyone there, Justine." Luke looked at his sister as if she was crazy.

"I saw someone in the hallway dressed in a black robe and there was a hood covering the face! I know I saw it! I saw the same figure last night in the hotel and then again outside the restaurant!" Justine was almost screaming at this point because she was scaring herself. She couldn't believe no one else had seen it. Even last night when she asked them about the black figure across the street, they acted then like they didn't see it. "I know it was there!"

"Justine, I don't know what you saw, but you definitely think you saw something," her dad said reassuringly. He needed to calm her down. They were standing in the middle of the hotel lobby and her voice was getting louder and louder.

"Okay, I believe you saw a person in the hallway. But that person is gone now and you will probably never see it again. Take some deep breaths and try to calm down. Please let me know immediately if you see that figure again, Justine."

"I will, Dad, I promise." Justine said as she started to breathe deeply. Whether or not she saw a figure dressed in black, she needed to try to forget it so she and her family could go sightseeing. "I'm okay now, Dad. Let's figure out where we're going to go today."

As they stood there, the smell of breakfast wafted passed them.

"Yum. Do you smell that? I almost forgot how hungry I am." Dad said rubbing his stomach. "Let's go get something to eat and talk about our schedule for the day."

"Great idea, Dad," Luke said as he turned to find out from where the delicious smells were coming.

They followed the smells to the hotel restaurant. It was a lovely spot. There were expansive windows all along two sides and lots of green planters strategically placed. They were shown to a table near the windows where they had a great view of the Thames. Breakfast was a buffet, so after they ordered their drinks, they all grabbed a plate and filled it with English breakfast foods. While they ate breakfast, they watched the boat traffic traveling up and down the river. Then Dad pulled the guide book out of his backpack.

"Here is a map of London. Let's look at the tours that are offered and decide which one sounds interesting."

"Let me see that map, Dad," Justine said as she reached for the book.

"Just one-minute, young lady," her dad replied holding the book away from her. "I'm going to place it in the middle of the table so we can all see it."

They studied the listed tours to see what sights were included in each tour. Finally, Luke pointed to one.

"Let's take the Palace Tour. It has a lot of places I would really like to see."

"Let me see that book," Justine said as she studied the names of the places on the tour. "If we went on that tour, we would see: Westminster Abbey, The Tower of

London, St. Paul's Cathedral, and Buckingham Palace. Alright, Luke actually has a good idea!"

"Great, then it's settled!" Dad grabbed the book and highlighted the tour so they wouldn't forget which one they had chosen. After Dr. Ross had paid for their breakfast, they all went out to the lobby to find the concierge so they could sign up for the tour. As Dr. Ross was completing the registration, he found out the tour also included a cruise of the Thames River. The tour would start out on a double-decker bus which would pick them up right outside the hotel.

# CHAPTER 5

# A DAY OF SIGHTSEEING

It was a beautiful morning, just the right kind of day to see the sights around London. They boarded the bus and decided to sit on the top deck so they would have a great view of the city. The first site was Westminster Abbey. Justine and Luke marveled at the architecture of the building. The building loomed over them as they sat in the bus listening to the guide. The guide explained the history of the Abbey and mentioned some of the names of famous people buried there.

From the Abbey, they could see Big Ben towering over the city which was the next stop. The three of them decided this would be a good place to get off the bus and tour this historical landmark. They found the stairs that led to the top of the clock and began the climb. They were breathing rather heavily as they neared the top of the tower. Once at the top, they entered the viewing area. It was so exciting to see London from this vantage point.

When they arrived back on the sidewalk, they waited for the next bus so they could continue the tour. There was room on the top deck so they sat there again. The next area was Piccadilly Circle and St. Paul's Cathedral. They found out that Admiral Nelson and Wellington were buried there. Also, it had been the site of Princess Diana's wedding.

Next on the tour was the Tower of London, home to the Crown Jewels. They learned from the guide that the jewels were protected by the famous group called the "Beefeaters". When they heard that, they both looked at each other and laughed since that seemed like a strange name for a group of people.

Then the bus took them to the dock where they were to board the river cruise on the Thames River. They climbed aboard the boat and decided to sit in the middle so they could view both sides of the shoreline. The cruise took them by Shakespeare's Globe Theater and traveled under the London Bridge. It docked at a pier near Buckingham Palace where they boarded another bus which took them to the Palace.

"I can't wait to see the changing of the guard." Justine was so excited that she started to push her way through the crowd. But her father grabbed her before she disappeared.

"Now just hold on, young lady! I don't want to lose either of you in this crowd. Let's all try to get to a place where we can see, together."

"Okay, Dad, but let's hurry so we don't miss anything!"

The three of them started to look for a good vantage point where they could see the ceremony. They found a small opening in the crowd and squeezed through. It ended up to be a great spot, right in front of the gates to the Palace.

When the ceremony had ended, they found their way back to the bus stop so they could return to the hotel. It had been a long, enjoyable day and they were all very tired.

"Wow, what a great day!" Luke said as he sat down on the bus.

"I can't believe we saw so many sites in one day!" Justine added excitedly.

"That was the way to see the city," Dr. Ross replied. "I'm sure glad we discovered this tour this morning. Way to go, team!"

"Me, too! I can't imagine trying to see all of that in one day on foot!" Justine stated.

When they got back to the hotel, Dr. Ross asked, "What do you say we look for some place to eat? All of that sightseeing has made me hungry!"

"Great idea!" Luke chimed in.

Just then, Justine heard someone say, "We need to hurry! Time is running out!" She looked around and there wasn't anyone standing near them. "Did you hear that? "Justine asked with a quiver in her voice.

"Hear what?" Luke asked. "I didn't hear a thing except my stomach growling!"

"I didn't hear anything either, Justine." Her dad stated with some concern. "Are you okay?"

"Oh, great! First I'm seeing things and now I'm hearing things." Justine didn't understand what was going on either and was getting very concerned. "I know I heard a voice! It sounded like a woman's voice. She said, 'We need to hurry! Time is running out!'"

"Running out for what, exactly?" Luke asked.

"I don't know, she didn't say," Justine replied with frustration.

"Maybe the voice was telling us that we need to hurry up and eat because we're all very hungry!" Luke laughed.

"Well, let's go get some dinner and maybe everyone will feel better."

And with that, Dr. Ross walked over to the front desk to inquire about a place to eat. They decided on a different restaurant than the night before which was also down the street from the hotel. This time, they wanted to try some traditional English foods. They were in London after all and they could get American food at home. Each one of them decided to get a different dish and then share the three meals. That way, they could sample more of the cuisine. Dr. Ross decided on Beef Wellington, Luke ordered Shepherd's Pie, and Justine wanted to try Bangers and mash. They decided of the three, the Beef Wellington was the best.

# CHAPTER 6

## JUSTINE'S GOING CRAZY

When dinner was over, the three tired sightseers started back to the hotel. Justine hadn't heard or seen anything the whole time they were eating dinner, so she had relaxed a little and figured it was all in her mind. On the way back, their dad's cell phone rang.

He grabbed the phone and checked the caller ID. "It's your mother! Hello. How are you? Oh wow! You're on your way here and will be here in the morning? That's great! Do you want us to meet you at the airport? Okay. We'll wait for you at the hotel. No, we did London today. But we will wait for you before we do anything else. Love you, too. See you tomorrow. Have a safe flight!" Dr. Ross put his phone back in the holder on his belt.

"Hey, Dad. Did we hear that right? Mom's going to be here tomorrow?" Luke asked excitedly.

"Yes, you heard right! Things worked out with that case she was handling and she got done earlier than expected. She'll get to the London airport tomorrow morning around 8:00. She's going to meet us at the hotel."

"Wow, I can't believe that she is actually going to join us on our vacation!" Justine yelled as she spun around in the sidewalk. "I can't wait for tomorrow morning!"

"Okay, kids, let's just get back to the hotel so we can get some sleep."

"Okay, Dad," both kids chimed in together.

They started down the street toward the hotel. As they walked, Justine had a strange feeling they were being followed. But every time she turned around to look, nothing was there. Was she starting to go crazy? She still couldn't believe she was the only one who could see the figure in black or hear the woman's voice. And now to have the feeling someone or something was following them was beginning to creep her out! When she saw the hotel, she took off at a run and got inside as fast as she could. She heard some huffing and puffing behind her and turned around to see her dad and brother out of breath.

"Justine, what's wrong?" Her dad asked as he bent over and tried to catch his breath. "You took off like you'd seen a ghost or something!"

"I know you both think I'm crazy, but I felt like something was following us on the way back from the restaurant."

"I know you're crazy! I've been saying that my whole life!" Luke replied with confidence.

"Justine, you're not crazy. But it does seem hard to believe that we are being watched," Dr. Ross said as he tried to console his daughter. "No one actually knows us in England. Maybe you're so excited about being here that your mind is playing tricks on you."

"I know what I saw and heard and I'm not crazy!" Justine yelled.

"Okay, let's get up to the room and get some rest. Everything will look better in the morning." Her dad hoped.

# CHAPTER 7

# THREE BECOMES FOUR

The alarm went off and everyone jumped out of bed. They all knew that Mom would be at the hotel in about two hours. Justine looked through her suitcase to find a nice outfit to wear since she wanted to look good for her mom. Luke grabbed whatever was the easiest which ended up to be the clothes he had worn the day before.

"Luke, you're not going to wear that outfit, are you? You wore that yesterday. And besides, you smell!" Justine proceeded to hold her nose to further show her disgust.

"Hey, what's wrong with it? Anyway, it saves on washing!"

"Luke, I agree with Justine," Mr. Ross added. "Please change into something clean."

"But if I look like this, Mom will know that we can't get along without her!" Luke retorted.

"I don't care! Just change your clothes!" Dr. Ross was in no mood for any problems this morning. "We need to finish getting dressed, clean up the room so it looks half-way decent, and then have breakfast."

Justine and Luke were finally dressed, both in a clean outfit. They each straightened their beds and picked up any clothes on the floor. Justine combed her hair and then put it in a ponytail. And of course, she had to wear the necklace so she could show her mother.

"I'm done, Dad," Justine offered.

"Me, too," Luke added.

"Great! Now let's get downstairs and have some breakfast. Your mom will be here in about an hour."

They decided to eat in the hotel restaurant again. They grabbed some tourist information to pour over while they ate breakfast. As soon as they had ordered, they opened the brochures to read about sites to see.

"Tell your dad you want to go see Stonehenge today."

"What, what did you say?" Justine asked. Luke and her dad both looked at her puzzled. Then she realized that neither her dad nor her brother had made that statement. It was the voice she had been hearing.

"Why should we go to Stonehenge?" Justine inquired of the voice.

"That's a great idea, Justine!" Dr. Ross nodded in agreement. "Stonehenge it is."

"What? I didn't say I wanted to go. I was asking why we should go."

"Asking why?" Her dad wondered.

"Oh, never mind. You wouldn't understand." She didn't want to tell them that she had heard the voice again. They already thought she was crazy. "I don't think we ought to go there, Dad," Justine pleaded. She wasn't sure why she had been asked to suggest it and was now very wary of the idea.

"Nonsense, it's settled! Stonehenge it is!" Dr. Ross closed the brochures since the decision was made.

"Great!" Luke said with great excitement. "I've always wanted to go there. It looks so cool! We learned about it at school. That place is nearly 5000 years old! And besides, don't you remember talking about it on the plane, Justine? We both decided it was one place we really wanted to go while we're in England."

"But, Dad!" Justine was now concerned that this was a bad idea.

Just then, they heard a familiar voice.

"There you are! I've been looking for you three everywhere!" It was Mom! They hadn't noticed the time. Justine and Luke leapt from the table and ran over to hug her. Dr. Ross gave her a welcome kiss. When they sat back down at the table, they all started talking simultaneously. "Hey, you're all talking at the same time and I can't follow any of your conversations. Drew, why don't you start?" Dr. Ross filled her in on the tour they had taken, with Justine and Luke adding their two cents, and also about the trip planned for the day.

# CHAPTER 8

# THE TOUR GETS UNDERWAY

Everything was ready. Dr. Ross, Luke, and Justine had all packed for the day prior to Mom's arrival even though they really didn't know where the day would take them. They had packed water bottles, snacks, sunscreen, Chapstick, and jackets. Mom had also packed a small bag for a day trip before she left home. She had the rest of her luggage delivered to the room.

"Ross, party of four for the tour to Stonehenge." They all looked up and noticed a man dressed in a blue shirt and khaki pants. On the shirt was the logo, "Stonehenge Tours".

"We're the Ross family," Dr. Ross blurted out as he got to his feet.

Justine and Luke grabbed their bags and headed toward the door. Dr. and Mrs. Ross followed behind them, his arm around his wife's waist.

"Follow me, please," the guide announced as they neared the door. "The bus is right outside the door to the left."

They looked around and saw a bright red double-decker bus parked on the side of the street. They boarded the bus, climbed the stairs to the second level, and sat about half-way back. The bus didn't seem to be very crowded. Then their guide made an announcement over the speakers.

"I want to welcome all of you to Stonehenge Tours. My name is Rob and I will be your guide today. We will be stopping at two more hotels to gather some more people for this trip. So, sit back and enjoy London. I will begin the formal tour once we are on our way to Stonehenge. We will be traveling by way of Oxford."

"Hey, Mom, you may get to see some of the sites we visited yesterday." Luke was excited to be traveling through parts of London on the way to the two other hotels.

"I wish I could have been there with you yesterday so I didn't have to just drive by them," Mom answered.

"I wish you could have been there, too! You would have loved seeing Buckingham Palace and the changing of the guard. That was sooo cool!" Justine was thinking about the great vantage point they had found.

"Well, I'm here now so I won't have to miss anything else!"

The bus arrived at the first hotel. Rob got off and entered the building. Everything in London was so much older than anything back home. If only the buildings could talk, that would have been a great history lesson.

Rob came back with about ten people following him. They all boarded the bus. Most of the people remained on the first level. The bus started up and Rob made the same announcement he had made earlier for the benefit of the new passengers.

"Look, Mom! There's Big Ben!" Justine pointed it out to her Mom.

"And Westminster Abbey," Luke chimed in.

The bus pulled to a stop in front of another hotel. "This is way cooler than I had imagined, Dad! When we talked at home about taking a side trip to Stonehenge, I never thought I would actually be going there! There are some great legends connected with that place. I wonder if we'll see any ghosts," Luke said as he turned toward Justine waving his arms. "Whooooooo!"

"Stop that! You know there's no such thing as ghosts," Justine asserted.

"Don't be so sure of yourself, Justine. You never know!"

"Okay you two." Dr. Ross thought he ought to jump in before the conversation got out of hand. "I think the rest of the tour group just boarded the bus which means we'll be on our way. Please listen to the tour guide. I'm sure he'll relay a lot of information to us as we travel to Stonehenge."

"I bet I could be the tour guide! I sure have a lot of information in my head that I learned in British literature last semester." Luke was pretty confident that he was the knowledgeable person on the bus.

"I'm not sure you have anything in that head of yours!" Justine countered.

# CHAPTER 9

# STONEHENGE

The tour was finally underway. The bus departed London with four excited passengers onboard. The whole trip would take about two and a half hours. The first stop was Oxford. The tour would stop there for a short break and then on to Stonehenge.

When they arrived in Oxford, the passengers got off the bus to do a little shopping, grab something to eat, or take a restroom break. Justine decided she had to go to the bathroom and told her mom and dad that she would return shortly.

On the way to the restroom, she felt that someone was behind her. She decided not to turn around and started to walk faster. She could see the sign for the restroom and knew she was close. Then she heard that voice again.

"Justine, you are close now. When you arrive at Stonehenge, I will give you some instructions. Please follow them. We desperately need your help."

Now she took off at a run and didn't stop until she was in the restroom. Once inside she quickly turned around to see if anyone was following her and didn't see anyone. Her hands clasped the sides of her face and she looked around the restroom to see if anyone was there. The ladies who were in the restroom stared at her. One of them came over to her and asked if there was anything wrong and could she be of some assistance. Justine looked at her and shook her head no. Now she knew there was something going on of which only she was aware. She was scared but at the same time curious to see what the voice was going to say next. What would those instructions be? Why had this "person" chosen her? And why so secretive? She took a deep breath and decided she would act as if nothing had happened. She wasn't going to tell her family any of this and just wait until Stonehenge to see what was going to happen next.

She returned to the bus and greeted her family as if nothing had happened.

"Hi. Well, I feel better now. What did everyone else do while I was gone?" Justine asked nonchalantly.

"Well," her mom replied, "I went into a little shop and got this journal. I thought it might come in handy as we document this trip. It fits very nicely in my purse."

"Good idea, Mom. That way we will be able to remember all the things we do on this trip." Justine was trying not to let anyone know that she was still scared.

Then Dr. Ross interrupted, "We need to get back on the bus. They're waiting for us."

There weren't any seats on the top of the bus so the family found four seats on the lower level. For the rest of the trip, Justine sat there quietly and just listened to all the conversations going on around her. She listened to see if she heard the "voice" again but didn't hear it among all of the other voices.

"Look, there it is!" Luke punched her in the arm with excitement.

"Ow!" and Justine looked up. There in the distance were the stone columns of Stonehenge. She saw a sign that indicated they were on a stretch of road named A303.

As they neared the structure, the guide came back on the speaker. "Ladies and gentlemen, we are almost at our destination. There are a few things I would like to say before we start the walking tour."

Justine stared out into the distance straining to see if there was any movement that might indicate someone was there to meet them. She could see the whole monument from the road and it looked very solemn there in the middle of the field. Then she focused back in and heard the guide finish up with, "You used to be able to explore the whole site, but the police had a fence placed around it due to the actions of some of the travelers. I ask that you remain seated until the bus stops completely. Once off the bus, please make your way to that large stone called the Heel Stone. I will meet you there. That is where our tour will start."

They left their bags on the bus except Mrs. Ross took her purse because that was something she never left behind. Then they proceeded to follow the tour guide.

# CHAPTER 10

## THE VOICE REVEALED

Everyone gathered around the stone and the guide started the tour.

"Here you will find that this prehistoric megalithic site dates back 4000 years and was created out of two kinds of stone: sarsen and bluestone. The sarsens used in the central part of the structure are much larger with the bluestones forming the outer circle. Please follow me and we will walk up what is now called the Avenue to the structure itself. Once we arrive at the outer circle, I will continue the tour."

The tour group followed the guide along the bank toward what looked like the entrance. He gathered the group near a large stone which was rusty red in color. The Ross family ended up in the back of the tour group and Justine was having a hard time seeing over the heads of everyone.

He began again, "Here is the northeast entrance to Stonehenge. There is also one on the south side. This rusty red stone here which lies in the entrance is known as the Slaughter Stone. The color has been caused over time by rainwater acting on iron in the stone."

"Mom and Dad, let's move over there. I can't see what the guide is talking about since we're in the back. That way we can all see better," Justine asked as she began to walk around the right side of the group. Her parents, and Luke, followed.

As they were standing there listening to the guide, Justine heard the voice talking to her again. But this time it was quiet, almost a whisper.

"Justine, please just listen and don't make any sudden movements or say anything to indicate that I am here. Just blink if you understand." Justine held her breath and blinked once. "Great, I was whispering so as not to frighten you. Now I will talk a little louder so you can hear me. My name is Gretchen. The necklace you're wearing allows you to see and hear me, but only you. I am a seeker. When my kingdom needs something that we can't grow or create, they send me, or someone like me, to find it. Sometimes that means I need to leave the safety of our realm and travel to yours." At this point, Justine's eyes grew very large and she continued staring at the guide.

"Hey, are you okay? You look a little pale and you have a distant look on your face," her mom said concerned.

"Huh, oh, I'm okay. I was just listening to the guide!"

"That was a little too close," Gretchen replied. "Great comeback. Okay, this may all sound a little strange..."

"A **little** strange!" Justine blurted out without realizing it.

"Justine! Please be quiet while the guide is talking."

"I'm sorry, Dad, I don't know what came over me!"

"As I was saying, all of this is not going to sound possible. But you need to believe me. The life of the king is at stake." Justine nodded and coughed so no one would notice. "I said that I am a seeker. So please know that I have been sent to bring your family to my kingdom, especially your father." At that point, Justine turned around to see who was talking to her, and still couldn't see anyone. "Our king is very ill and we believe it is due to his heart. We learned that your family would be in England and that your dad is a famous heart surgeon. So, it is now my job to bring you and your family to our kingdom. It would be great if you could find a way to excuse yourself from the group and follow my voice. Then I can reveal myself to you and you will know I am real."

Justine wasn't sure what to think. At first, she just thought she was going crazy. But now, this voice was telling her about a kingdom and a king? What next, was a knight going to show up with his sword and force her to follow Gretchen. At least the voice now has a name! Okay, she'll bite but only because she was very curious to finally get the chance to see the person behind the voice.

"Mom, I'm going to walk over to that stone. It looks like it has some markings on it and I want to get a closer look." Justine thought that sounded logical.

"Okay, dear, but don't go too far."

"Okay, Mom."

"Very good, now follow my voice, please." Well at least Gretchen was polite. "You should stand where your mother can see you. Then she will not get nervous and I will stand behind this massive stone."

While Justine listened and kept her eyes in the direction of the voice, she noticed that her necklace started glowing and as it did a figure started to appear in front of her. She gasped as the face took form and she could actually see Gretchen. She had to cover her own mouth because she felt like screaming.

"Oh wow!" Then Justine started mumbling to herself, "There you are, you're real, you're a real person, you've got hair and everything and you're wearing a black cloak. Wow! That explains everything..."

"Please focus, Justine. We do not have much time. I have been in communication with another seeker and he is telling me that the king is much worse and we need to get there as soon as possible."

"Get where, exactly?" Justine looked around and couldn't see anything but the stones of Stonehenge.

"I will show you as soon as we can get your family all in one place." And with that Gretchen lifted her hand and pointed toward the inner circle of stones. "We need to enter over there, through that stone."

"Through the what? I don't think I heard you correctly."

"That stone is a portal to my kingdom, and very few know about it. Now, please call your family over here and act like you want to show them these figures on the stone. I will take it from there." Gretchen disappeared but Justine could still here her voice, "Please hurry."

Justine walked over to where her family was standing listening to the guide. "Mom, Dad, Luke, I need to show you these neat markings I found. I really need you to help me figure out what they are supposed to be.

"Justine, please be quiet. We are trying to hear what the guide is saying." Her mom was a little perturbed that Justine didn't seem interested in the historical information the guide was relaying.

"This won't take very long. You won't miss anything. Please...! You'll be sorry if you don't at least look at them. They are so cool!" Then Justine reached for her mom's hand to lead her away from the group. She knew if she got her mother to go with her, then her dad and Luke would follow.

"Okay, Justine, I'll go with you. Where are these markings?"

Justine sighed with relief and led them over to the big stone where she and Gretchen had been talking. When the family got there, Gretchen was standing near the stone but still only visible to Justine.

"Here are the markings! Look at them, aren't they cool? See how many of them there are! I wonder what they say."

Then Justine heard Gretchen say something in a strange language. At the same time, one of the other tourists walked over to the stone where the family was standing. Justine started to get nervous, but then realized from his actions that he didn't even see them. Somehow, they had become invisible, and not only that, her parents and Luke seemed to be under some kind of spell.

"Justine, please follow me, and help guide your family." Gretchen started walking toward the stone she had identified earlier. Justine walked behind her family making sure they didn't run into anything or stumble and fall. Gretchen arrived at the stone and again said something that Justine couldn't quite make out. Gretchen motioned to Justine to move toward the stone and Justine noticed that her family was also walking in that direction. Then one by one they disappeared into the stone. "Don't be afraid, Justine, I will be right behind you!"

Justine was sure she would hit the stone and not go anywhere. She put her hands out in front of her to help with the jolt she was sure was coming. But as she did, instead of hitting the stone, they disappeared into the stone and her body followed. When she stopped, she shook her head and then it hit her. She had just passed through a massive stone and nothing hurt! She looked around and realized she wasn't at Stonehenge anymore! The landscape around her was now totally different from where she had been before. She could see a forest all around her. The trees were immense and so green. She panicked for a moment and looked for her family. They were standing a few feet to her left and looked to be okay. She heard a noise, turned around and saw Gretchen coming through the portal.

"Where are we?" Justine directed the question to Gretchen. She knew she had read about things like this but only in fiction and pinched herself to make sure she wasn't dreaming. "Is this real? Did we just walk through that very large stone?"

"Yes, Justine. That stone is the portal to my kingdom."

"I really thought you were just kidding!"

"I need your help again. I am going to remove the spell and you and I are going to have to explain this to them in such a way that they do not panic!"

"We? I don't understand all of this myself!"

Then Gretchen said something and Justine noticed her family began to lose the glazed look in their eyes.

"Where in heaven's name are we?" Justine's dad stated as he looked around him. "How did we get here? And who are you? Where is Stonehenge?"

"Dr. Ross, I am Gretchen from the Kingdom of Wiltshire, and I was sent to bring you and your family here to help the king who is very ill."

"What are you talking about? King, kingdom? There's no such thing. Those are terms the people of England used long ago! Where is Stonehenge? Where is our tour guide? I demand answers and I want them now!"

"Dad," Justine interrupted, "do you remember in London when I told you I saw and heard someone and you all thought I was crazy. Well, that was Gretchen! Look at her clothes. Didn't I say I had seen someone dressed in black and was wearing a black robe?"

"Yes, I vaguely remember you mentioning something but I really wasn't paying much attention. So that really happened, that wasn't your imagination running away with you? Well, why could Justine see you and not us?"

"Dr. Ross, do you remember a necklace Justine found in the limo that picked you up at the airport? The moment she put it on she was able to see and hear me. But only she had that ability. That is why she continued to see someone dressed in black. The necklace has an amulet that allows us to communicate with people from outside our kingdom."

"Okay, that may explain why we all thought Justine was going crazy, but that still doesn't explain why you brought us here."

"I'll tell you in the carriage on the way to the castle. We must hurry. The king is very ill."

Just then, a team of four black horses appeared out of nowhere pulling a beautiful white carriage with gold inlays and behind it six soldiers followed on horseback. The soldiers were wearing green and purple uniforms and brandishing very shiny swords on their left side.

"Please get in, we can waste no more time!" Gretchen pointed to the carriage and the driver of the carriage opened the door for them.

# CHAPTER 11

## THE ROYAL FAMILY

As the Ross family rode to the castle, Justine and her family listened intently while Gretchen described the Kingdom of Wiltshire to them and the castle walls that surrounded it. She told them about their beloved King William and Queen Marianne who had ruled for 10 years and of their four children, John aged 19, James aged 18, Madison aged 12, and Bethany aged 10. She talked about the village and the townspeople and that the kingdom had lived in peace with their surrounding neighbors for the past ten years.

They rounded a bend, climbed a small hill and there on the side of a mountain in front of them was the massive, pristine, white, stone castle Gretchen called Wiltshire.

"Oh wow! Doesn't that remind you of Camelot!" Justine was in awe of the sight that loomed in front of her.

"I've never seen anything like it on all my travels," her father replied.

"This is sooo awesome! I can't wait to go across the drawbridge and see what's inside those walls!" Luke blurted out.

"I must be dreaming," Mrs. Ross said bewildered.

The castle walls, of which there appeared to be many, had turrets atop the front gate manned by several soldiers. From the hill where they had stopped momentarily, it looked as though there was a whole town located within the walls. Toward the back of the castle, they could see octagonal towers atop of what looked like a very large residence.

The carriage approached its destination with the precious travelers inside. There was a large moat around the castle and the drawbridge had been lowered to allow them entrance. Justine marveled at the thickness of the walls as they traversed the bridge and went under the enormous gates. They went through an outer wall and then an inner wall.

"Why are there two walls?" Justine inquired.

"They are for protection. This is called the "Gatehouse". If an enemy would breach the outer wall, they then would need to breach the inner one as well."

"That makes sense." Luke added.

They traveled down several streets in what seemed to be an outer courtyard. Here they saw horses and pigs grazing as well as lots of houses. Once past that, they moved on to a magnificent stone courtyard filled with people.

"And here you have the inner courtyard where the people focus on the day-to-day of castle life." Gretchen informed them.

The people were scurrying around greeting each other and visiting the street vendors. There were people playing instruments and others dancing.

However, this didn't look like the England they had read about in school or would have expected. There appeared to be some modern conveniences mixed in with the old. There were wires overhead that looked to be electrical and a huge fountain in the middle of the square with running water. As they looked around, there seemed to be some dark areas of the square illuminated by light bulbs! They all let out a uniform gasp when they saw a bicycle whiz by.

"Did you see that?" Justine queried.

And the rest of the family replied "Yes!" simultaneously!

Directly behind the courtyard was an enormous palace that had been built within the walls of the castle. That looked to be the residence of the royal family. It was more elaborate than the surrounding buildings and had a banner flying over the main door with what appeared to be a golden dragon on it. As the carriage approached, the villagers all stopped in their tracks. They watched as the carriage passed them for they knew the seeker had successfully returned from her quest.

The carriage pulled up in front of a large wooden door beneath the banner. The soldiers who had been following the carriage now dismounted and took up their positions on either side of the doorway, three on each side, standing at attention. The door squeaked open to reveal a welcoming committee. The queen and what appeared to be her eldest son approached the carriage with excitement!

"Gretchen, I see you have returned with our doctor!" Queen Marianne stated with delight. "I am so proud of you!"

"Thank you, your majesty. It took me a little longer than expected. I hope the king is still with us," Gretchen asked in a hopeful manner.

"Yes, he is. But I think he will need medical attention very soon."

Gretchen motioned to the family to exit the carriage. "Your majesty, may I present Dr. Ross and his family." As the family stepped down out of the carriage Gretchen continued, "Dr. Ross, this is Queen Marianne. Your majesty, this is his wife, Stephanie, their son, Luke, and daughter, Justine. Dr. Ross, the queen will escort you to the bed chamber of the King, and their eldest son, John, will see to the rest of the family."

The queen took Dr. Ross' hand, "Thank you so much for coming to the Kingdom of Wiltshire. We are very happy you are here." Then she turned around and led him through the doorway into the residence.

"Well, we didn't have much of a choice in the matter," he stated. Then he turned around to make sure his family was being attended to.

"I am very sorry for that," the queen replied. "The King grew sick and we were in need of a special physician. So, Gretchen was sent out to your world to find a doctor, and if possible, a heart doctor. Please, follow me."

As she led him into the main hallway, Dr. Ross couldn't help notice how regal the queen appeared in her stature. She glided into the palace as if on a moving walkway and clasped her hands directly in front of her at waist level as she walked. She had long wavy blonde hair which reminded him of Justine's hair, but her eyes were blue and Justine's were brown. When she turned to address him, her whole body turned in a single motion. She was wearing a flowing purple gown and a small tiara.

"We will need to ascend the stairway to get to the bedchamber," the queen announced. Dr. Ross looked around and before him were white marble floors which led to a centralized grand staircase. The walls appeared to be covered in red velvet tapestries and on each one hung a portrait framed in gold which looked to be of former kings. They proceeded up the staircase to the landing which led to two more sets of stairs. They took the stairs on the left to the second floor. Once at the top of the stairs, the queen led him down a long hallway to the door at the end and stopped.

"King William is in his bed resting and has been anticipating your arrival. Please wait here while I go in and announce you are here." The Queen opened the door and disappeared into the room.

Dr. Ross was left standing in the hallway. He looked around him and still couldn't believe he was standing in a palace! Then he asked himself out loud, "What am I doing here? How did she know she needed a heart doctor?" As he stood there, it suddenly dawned on him that he didn't know what had become of his family. Were they safe? Then he heard a voice from the other end of the hallway, "Hey, Dad, isn't this cool?" It was Luke's voice. "Can you believe we're actually in a castle?" He looked up and there they were, Luke and Justine. He knew his wife couldn't be far away. He breathed a sigh of relief. "Thank God, they're okay,' he sighed.

Just then, the door opened. "You may come in now, Dr. Ross. The King will see you." The Queen motioned for him to enter the King's chambers.

# CHAPTER 12

## KING WILLIAM

Dr. Ross entered the room not knowing what to expect. What would he be able to do for the King? Not having any of the equipment he utilized every day back home was going to make a difference in how well he could diagnose much less treat the king.

"Dr. Ross..., Dr. Ross, is there something wrong? The Queen asked.

"What, huh, oh I'm sorry. I was lost in thought," he replied.

"Dr. Ross, this is my husband, King William."

The King was lying in a huge ornate, wooden bed with a purple velvet blanket. He was propped up on several pillows. He looked to be about the same age as Dr. Ross; Dr. Ross being 45. The King's hair had some gray at the temples mixed in with his auburn locks and in his beard. He was a nice-looking man and appeared to be somewhat healthy. But appearances can often be deceiving.

"So happy to meet you, your majesty. I wish it was under different circumstances. I'm not sure how to address you, sir. Should I bow, shake your hand...?"

"Please, we aren't going to deal with formalities right now," the King said in a whisper. "I am glad you have arrived safely."

"As soon as William started having problems, we sent our best seeker to your world to find a doctor, preferably a heart doctor if possible," the Queen interjected. "That is why you are here. I hope you will be able to help him."

"But why a heart doctor? What led you to believe that was the kind of doctor you needed?" he said puzzled.

"I will do my best to explain that in a moment, but right now, will you please examine him?" the Queen pleaded.

And with that, Dr. Ross moved closer so he could assess his patient. "How old are you, sir?"

"William is forty years old," the Queen answered for the King. "His birthday was yesterday. But, of course, the kingdom could not celebrate due to his illness."

"I am fine, Marianne. I can answer for myself," King William said. "Would you summon Dr. Lange, please? I would like to have him here so he can advise Dr. Ross regarding my condition."

"Yes, William," and the Queen left the room.

"Dr. Lange? I don't understand. Who is he?" he asked the King.

"He should be here shortly and he can answer any questions you may have."

"Well, then, I guess I should begin the examination. Would you mind answering some questions for me?"

"Not at all, ask what you wish."

"When did you first notice that things were different, you didn't feel normal?"

"About a month ago," the King whispered.

"How have you been feeling, can you describe what's been happening? Have your symptoms been continuous or do they come and go?"

Then Dr. Ross was startled by the door suddenly opening. In walked the Queen followed by a man who he assumed to be Dr. Lange.

The man walked right over to Dr. Ross and extended his hand, "Dr. Ross, I'm so excited to finally meet you! I had heard and read so much about you before I left England! Oh, I'm sorry, I'm Dr. Lange. I was a general practitioner in Oxford and prior to that lived in Boston."

"Happy to meet you, Dr. Lange."

"Please, it's Adam, Adam Lange."

"Adam, it's nice to meet you. I'm Andrew, well just Drew." Then Dr. Ross asked, "What are you doing here? You have a stethoscope around your neck! And you're carrying a blood pressure cup! When, how, I don't understand?"

"Well, long story short, I was brought here just like you, by a seeker about three years ago. They needed a doctor at the time to tend to one of the princesses. I needed to be here about three weeks to ensure the illness was gone and no one else became infected. But once I was finished, I made the decision to stay since I had grown to love it here. I don't have any family at home so it worked out. I can explain everything, but you might need these to begin your examination," Dr. Lange threw in and handed him the two items.

Dr. Ross took both and used them to listen to the King's heart and check his blood pressure. "Dr. Lange, Adam, maybe you can answer some questions for me about the King's condition. He is out of breath and therefore having trouble talking. Would that be okay with you your majesty?"

The king consented to his request with a nod.

They moved to a corner in the room so they could discuss Dr. Lange's findings without disturbing the King. After consulting, Dr. Ross concurred that the king probably had a heart condition. His initial diagnosis was arrhythmia, but he needed to run more tests to make sure. And how was he going to do that when he needed more equipment?

# CHAPTER 13

## WHAT COMES NEXT?

"Adam, I need to know what equipment, if any, you currently have here." Dr. Ross was trying to ascertain what to do next given the circumstances.

"Well, I was able to bring some with me the first time I came here. Then, after I decided to stay, had to go back for more."

"You went back to get equipment after you first arrived here?" Dr. Ross was very surprised that Dr. Lange had traveled back and forth from one world to the next.

"Yes, one of the seekers was assigned to take me there and bring me back! You're not allowed to go through the portal without a seeker if you are returning. I think the seekers have some kind of magic that makes it possible. It felt very strange bringing all that equipment to Stonehenge with us. We had to travel at night so no one would see us. It's important the entrance remains a secret."

"How long did it take you to make the journey? How long would it take me if I needed more than you currently have here? And... how can we use some of the equipment when most, if not all of it, probably needs electricity to be able to function?"

"Oh, the journey doesn't take very long. Something happens when you go through the stones. They can return you to the day and time you left so that you're not missed. If that didn't happen, it would bring attention to the fact that you've been gone. And another important fact, if you go through the portal without a seeker, then you will lose all memory of ever being here. That's why it's necessary to return you to the moment you left. But it also depends on how many times you go through the portal. They can only turn back time when you initially go back through the portal. I'm the only one I know of that has ever returned. But time continues to move on this side of the stones at the usual pace. Oh, and yes, there is electricity here, believe it or not. That's another long story for another time."

Dr. Ross stood there trying to make sense of it all. But finally decided it didn't matter what would happen when he left as long as he could treat his patient now. "Okay, let's assess the situation, decide what tests I'll need to run in order to determine what the King's actual heart problem is, and then treat it. If additional equipment is needed, I guess I can return to London to see if I can locate what I need. London... I totally forgot! I was in London for a symposium? I'm supposed to be the guest speaker!"

"So sorry you had to leave. We will *try* to make sure you arrive in time for the symposium so as not to arouse suspicion. But for now, I'll take you to my office to show you what is currently in my inventory and go from there." Dr. Lange stated as he turned to leave.

"Excuse me, Drs., but before you depart, it is important the King know of your plan. Please inform his majesty what Dr. Ross thinks the problem to be and what the doctor needs to do to treat him. He also would like to know what he is to do while he waits for your decision," Queen Marianne said.

"I'm so sorry!" Dr. Ross replied. "I got so caught up in the moment that I forgot to apprise my patient of the situation. This is all **very** new to me!"

Dr. Ross approached the King's bed again and proceeded to relay the information about the needed equipment, the possible diagnosis, and the instructions for the King to follow while waiting for further tests. King William nodded to indicate he understood the instructions.

The Queen stood up and nodded to them as well. "Thank you both so much for offering to assist William and to help heal him. We appreciate it more than you know. I will make sure he follows your instructions while we await your decision. Please let us know if we can be of any help. Right now, I will go find your wife, Dr. Ross, to help her get settled."

Dr. Lange and Dr. Ross then left the King's bedroom to go to Dr. Lange's office.

# CHAPTER 14

## THE CHILDREN MEET

"You mean this whole room is for me!" Justine burst out very loudly. "It's so big! And look at that bed! I've always wanted a canopy bed!"

"Okay, Justine. Contain your excitement for a minute will ya!" Luke motioned to his sister to sit down and be quiet. "Thank you for your hospitality, Prince John."

"Thank you for your hospitality? Who are you trying to impress?" Justine punched her brother on the arm.

"Would you leave me alone!" Luke said as he punched her back.

"You two sound like our family!" Prince John stated. "We fight at times, well, at least when Mother and Father aren't looking."

"Oh, we're not fighting, are we Luke?"

"No, this is our normal conversation," Luke replied.

"Well, I really find that hard to believe, but I'll take you at your word." Prince John said in disbelief.

Prince John was not one to take things lightly. He was very reserved in his mannerisms. He knew he was next in line for the throne and it was important to him that he exhibit confidence in himself and his decisions. He wasn't sure what to make of these two young people who were now guests in his kingdom.

Three more children entered the room. Prince John introduced his brother, Prince James, and his sisters, Princesses Madison and Bethany to Luke and Justine. They were definitely members of the same family as they all looked very similar. Both John and James were taller than Luke and Luke measured about 5' 10". They both had auburn hair and brown eyes. However, the girls had long blonde hair and blue eyes.

"Justine, you look to be our sister!" Princess Madison declared.

"Aye, she does," James chimed in.

Justine looked up and noticed James smiling at her. She quickly looked away and felt her face grow warm. Then she nervously began a conversation with Princess Madison.

"How old are you, Princess Madison?"

"I am twelve. In nearly two months, I will be thirteen," she stated.

"And I am ten!" Princess Bethany interjected. She didn't want to be forgotten. "John is nineteen and James is eighteen."

"Well, I'm fifteen now but I will soon turn sixteen since my birthday is about a month away." Justine replied. "So nice to meet all of you."

"I can't believe we are all so close in age!" Luke said surprised.

"Luke, please follow me. I will show you to your bedchamber," Prince John said changing the subject. He proceeded toward the door and turned around to make sure Luke was behind him. Luke followed him out of the room as did Madison and Bethany.

"I want to see where Luke is going," Princess Madison said adoringly.

"So do I!" Princess Bethany threw in as she bounced through the door.

Justine started laughing at the girl's comments and turned back around. She noticed that Prince James was still standing in the room. He seemed to be much more relaxed than his brother and he walked over and sat down in a chair.

"Please sit down so we can talk."

Justine very casually walked over and sat down near the Prince.

"Where do you hail from?" he asked.

"We're from the United States, Indianapolis, Indiana, to be exact." She realized after she said it that he probably had no idea what she was talking about. "Um, I bet you may not have heard of any of these places. The United States wasn't even established until 1776. In the old days it was called, "The New World." It was discovered by Christopher Columbus. In fourteen hundred and ninety-two, Columbus sailed the ocean blue. Oh, sorry, I got a little carried away. By the way, what year is it here?"

"It's 1520," James responded as if she should have known that.

"Really! Oh wow! Really? That's hard to believe!" Justine was definitely surprised by his answer. That meant that her family had traveled over 500 years by just walking though a stone! "Do you do this a lot? Have visitors from other time periods?"

"Aye. This has been going on for about 150 years," Prince James said. "But of course, I have not been around to see it!" he said jokingly. Justine realized he had a sense of humor.

"Of course not. You couldn't have been! You're only eighteen, right? I mean, who could live that long?" Justine threw in.

"Not I, for sure!" Prince James stated emphatically. "What year is it where you hail from?"

"It's 2020! A 500-year difference! But standing here, in this room, it's like there's no difference at all."

"That is surprising! I am sure a lot has happened since the 1500's in your world. Things I think would be interesting to see someday. But for now, would you like to see more of the castle?" Prince James asked as he got up and moved toward the door. "And, it is just James when we are talking to each other."

"That would be fantastic, ...James" and she followed him out the door.

# CHAPTER 15

## STEPHANIE

Stephanie Ross certainly hadn't planned for a detour on their trip and now didn't know what to make of all of this. Prince John left her sitting in the Main Hall while he showed Justine and Luke to their quarters. She looked around trying to ascertain where her family had landed hoping to gain more information about the King and his family. She noticed the pictures on the walls surrounding the hall and got up to view the portraits.

She began with the one nearest to her. Underneath the picture was a gold name plate which read, King James, 1460-1510. She moved on to the next one and it was a portrait of the King who had preceded King James. As she moved around the hall, the pictures were a succession of Kings starting in the 1300's. The portraits indicated that there had been at least six kings prior to King William, some had very short terms as ruler. She moved to the middle of the hall to observe the pictures and noticed the family resemblances among them. Then she heard footsteps coming down the stairs.

"Mrs. Ross, I have finally located you! I was not told where Prince John had left you. I am so sorry for the confusion, but it was important that your husband attend to the King as soon as he arrived," the Queen said as she approached Mrs. Ross. "I hope you will feel at home here during your stay. Please come have some ale and sit with me for a little while?" And not waiting for a reply from Mrs. Ross, she rang a little bell that had been sitting on a table near her.

A servant entered the room immediately saying, "Yes, your grace, what may I do for you?"

"Cedric, would you please bring us some ale and bring it to the side table in the Great Hall?"

"Yes, your grace, right away," and Cedric left the hallway.

"Please, follow me to the Great Hall, Mrs. Ross," the Queen said as she turned to leave.

Stephanie walked behind the Queen through the hallway and into a very large room which she assumed to be the Great Hall. There was one enormous, very heavy rectangular wooden table sitting in front of a massive fireplace. It was surrounded by twenty-two chairs covered in the same red velvet she had seen in the main hall. The Queen walked toward a small alcove on the left side of the Great Hall where a smaller table had been placed with several chairs. She sat down on one of the chairs and motioned to Stephanie to sit across from her. At that moment, Cedric entered holding a tray which he placed on the table in front of the Queen. He placed a goblet in front of the Queen and then Mrs. Ross.

"How do you like the ale, Mrs. Ross? Do you find it to your liking?" the Queen asked impatiently. She was too concerned about the King to be sitting there sharing ale with Mrs. Ross. But she knew her place as Queen was to welcome guests into the castle so she would make the best of it.

"Oh, it's very good," she said as she choked a little. "It is very different than anything we have in my time period."

"Thank you, Cedric. You are dismissed." And Cedric bowed and left the room.

"These goblets are very heavy. What are they made from?"

"A seeker brought them to us through the portal. I think they are made from silver. Mrs. Ross, please tell me some things about you. How do you pass the time in your country?"

"I'm a prosecuting attorney," Stephanie answered. Then she noticed a puzzled look on the Queen's face. "Oh, sorry! I'm a lawyer, ... uh ... someone who helps bring those who do wrong to justice."

"What a noble calling! I admire people who help keep the world safe."

"Thank you. I wasn't able to come to London with the family because I had to complete a big case I had been working on for several months. But as it turned out the case finished before I had expected it to and I was able to surprise them in London. One of the sightseeing trips we took happened to be to Stonehenge and now we're here! Which my very logical self is still having a hard time wrapping my head around!

"I am very glad you and your family are here for the sake of the King. Your husband is speaking with our physician right now to decide what the next steps will be."

"Your physician?" Stephanie looked at her in disbelief. "You have a physician here in Wiltshire?"

"Aye, we do!" the Queen answered as if it should be common knowledge. "He has been with us for three years. One of our seekers brought him to us because Bethany was very sick and our healers could not make her well. One seeker, Gretchen, who brought your family here, thought it would be good to bring a doctor from your world to help her. We are very glad Gretchen made that suggestion because I am afraid we might have lost her had it not been for Dr. Lange. And so, that is how Dr. Lange came to be our family physician and he has been with us ever since."

"That is truly fascinating! I wonder why someone would chose to give up their life in our world to remain here? I would like to meet this Dr. Lange sometime."

"You will when the right time presents itself. But now, I need to make sure you are escorted to your bedchambers." Then the Queen rang the bell two times. This time a lady entered the room. "Adelaide, will you please show Mrs. Ross to her sleeping chambers and help her get settled?" Then addressing Mrs. Ross, "Adelaide will be your maid during your stay here. If you need anything, Adelaide will see to it."

"Thank you, your majesty."

When she got up to leave, Queen Marianne noticed she was holding a small bag. "What do you have in your hands?"

"This? Oh, it's called a purse. Many women in my time carry them. It holds items we might need while we are away from home. It has a long strap so I can put it over my head so I won't lose it!"

"That seems like a good thing to have. You may follow Adelaide now."

Then Adelaide led Stephanie from the Great Hall and up the large staircase to the room which was to be Mrs. Ross' bedchambers.

On the way to the room, Stephanie could hear voices behind her coming from one of rooms on the other end of the corridor. She thought one of the voices sounded like Drew so she turned around and walked toward them. There, in a room that looked like a doctor's office, was her husband talking to a man who she assumed was Dr. Lange. She walked rather quickly into the room to greet her husband.

"Drew, I'm so glad to see you!" She wrapped her arms around him not wanting to let go. "I haven't seen anyone in the family since we arrived," she said as tears started to stream down her face.

"Stephanie, I'm so sorry! Everything happened so fast I forgot to ask about your whereabouts. Please forgive me?" he gently asked.

She lowered her arms and grabbed his hand so she was assured he wasn't going anywhere. "Please don't leave me alone again. Everyone disappeared and I was left all by myself in the Main Hall. I didn't know where you had gone," and tears started to form again.

"I'm not planning on going anywhere. We're together now and that's all that matters." Drew gave her a kiss to help calm her.

Then realizing Dr. Lange was still standing there he said, "This is Dr. Adam Lange, physician to the royal family. Dr. Lange, this is my wife, Stephanie." Stephanie put out her hand so they could shake hands.

"Stephanie, I'm very happy to make your acquaintance. I knew of your husband's fame before I came to Wiltshire and am so honored to finally be able to meet him. I can't tell you how glad I am that he's here. I wasn't able to do what was needed for the King and I was afraid we were going to lose him. But your husband stepped right up, took charge, and I think there's a good chance the King is going to make it. Now the question is, what to do next."

"Stephanie, Dr. Lange has been here for three years and has collected quite a few medical items from back home and brought them here. But I'm afraid they aren't going to be enough. I'll need some specialized tests and equipment so I can accurately diagnose the problem and then, I hope, be able to treat the King." Dr. Ross was very concerned as to how this was all going to play out and he drifted off into his own thoughts.

"Mrs. Ross, I turned around and you had disappeared for a moment." Adelaide said as she entered the room.

"Oh, Drew, this is Adelaide, and she has been assigned to me by the Queen to be my maid while we're here. I really don't think that was necessary, but I didn't want to question the Queen's decision. Queen Marianne said she came to find me because she realized I was by myself. She asked me to drink some ale with her which was very nice even though I didn't much care for it. She asked Adelaide to take me to my room, I mean, our room. I'm assuming we have a bedroom together."

"Yes, mum. You will be in the same room as your husband," Adelaide replied.

"Well, that's very good to know," Mrs. Ross said with a sigh.

"Please follow me, Mrs. Ross, and I will show you to your room. It is only just down the hall." And with that, Adelaide turned and started down the hallway.

"Well, if you two will excuse me, I guess I need to go with Adelaide!" said Mrs. Ross as she excused herself from the conversation. Then she stopped and turned around. "Drew, I hope I will be able to see you soon. And another thing, have you seen either Luke or Justine lately?"

"No, sorry dear, I haven't, but I'm sure they're around here somewhere!" Then he returned to his conversation with Dr. Lange and Stephanie reluctantly followed Adelaide down the hall.

# CHAPTER 16

## THE PALACE

"I can't get over how big this place is!" Justine was in awe of the many rooms in the palace Prince James had already shown her on the tour. "How many rooms are in this palace?"

"I think there to be near twenty, but I do not visit all of them. I do not have reason to go to other parts of the palace or the castle. I am content to stay in the main rooms most of the time."

"Well, I hope I don't get confused and go the wrong direction sometime. I have a tendency to daydream and could very easily get lost."

"Pray, remain near the main stairway and you will always know where you are," Prince James said with assurance.

"Okay, thank you so much for showing me around. I really appreciate it. Oh, just curious about something. We noticed a person riding a bicycle through the courtyard when we first arrived. Would you mind telling me how that got here?"

"Oh, aye, the bicycle! You see, oft a seeker will travel through the portal and return with an item of interest from the future. Tis most splendid to see some of the things that have been "invented", I think that to be the term Dr. Lange uses, that we will not live to see."

"Do you ever want to travel through the portal to see the future for yourself." Justine knew that if she lived in this time period and had the opportunity to see the future, she would jump at the chance.

"My father tells us we need to learn to live in our own time and not covet the things we do not have. We do make use of what we receive from the future, like electricity. Life is much easier for us. But we dare not mention any of this to the Kings in the kingdoms around us for they would certainly want to take it for themselves, and may even lead to war. We have been at peace for the last ten years ever since my father became King and we do not want to see that destroyed."

"Oh, wow! I didn't even think of that. We don't have that problem back home. But I can see that it could be a problem here!"

"When we have visitors from the other kingdoms, we hide anything we have taken from your world so that they do not see it."

"Hey, what about the portal? Do they know about that?"

"No, that is a secret my kingdom has guarded for the past one hundred fifty years. It is hard for me to imagine what would happen if the other kings knew about it! We would go to war because we would not want to allow another king to have control over the portal. And what would happen in your world if they did?"

"That would be disaster!" Justine affirmed. "Your secret is safe with me!"

"That is good to know!" However, James knew that anyone who visited his kingdom would have no recollection of ever being there once they passed back through the portal to their own time without a seeker.

"But I have a question. You mentioned that this has been going on for the past one hundred and fifty years.

Why wasn't the portal used before then? This kingdom has obviously been here longer than that."

"That is true. It is told that during the early years before Wiltshire, it was used by sorcerers to travel between the worlds. I think it was used then as it is now, to bring things from the future. But also, to keep an eye on what the future might hold for us, to learn from the visits. Then, the portal was lost for a time and became a legend. One day, when Wiltshire was a young kingdom, a sorcerer came upon some writings that talked of a portal connected to a place called Stonehenge. They searched for it and discovered it quite by accident. After that, the sorcerer trained some young people of the kingdom to become seekers and now that gift has been handed down through the years. Gretchen is a descendent of those first seekers."

"That is so interesting! Do you have a sorcerer now?"

"Aye, we do. You will most definitely meet him while you are here." Prince James glanced out the window, "I did not realize so much time had passed. It is beginning to get dark outside now. Come, let us go find John and Luke and see what they have been doing. I think they may still be on the second floor with Madison and Bethany still following them." And Prince James led Justine back to the main hallway.

# CHAPTER 16

## DECISION MADE

"Dr. Ross, the Queen has been looking everywhere for you! You must come quickly! The King is struggling to breathe!" Adelaide escorted him down the hallway to the King's chambers followed by Dr. Lange.

As they opened the door, the Queen immediately got up from her chair and addressed Dr. Ross. "Dr. Ross, I'm so glad Adelaide found you. The King has gotten worse! What are we to do?"

"Let me examine him, please." And Dr. Ross moved quickly to the King's bedside. He checked his pulse and his blood pressure. Then he listened to the King's lungs and his heart. Although he didn't have very much to work with, Dr. Ross was able to stabilize the King so he was breathing more comfortably and then turned to the Queen. "He's stable now, but his blood pressure is elevated and so is his pulse. I now hear a fluttering or gurgling noise coming from his heart that I didn't notice before. I think he may have a heart infection which in turn could have damaged one of the valves. I don't know how this happened, could be family history or from an illness he has had. Dr. Lange has informed me that he administered an antibiotic to treat any infection he might have and has one more dose on hand. He showed me the medical items he has in his possession and I'm afraid he doesn't have the equipment necessary to treat the King at this point. We can give him the last dose of the antibiotic tonight and then the only thing I know to do is to get him to a hospital as quickly as possible. I don't see any way around it! I absolutely must take him back through the portal to the closest hospital where I will have all of the needed equipment. If I'm correct, I think he's going to need surgery."

"Surgery! Dr. Lange has explained the word surgery to me, but I hoped that would not be necessary." The Queen was caught off guard with this latest news and worked to pull herself together so she could help make the important decisions now needed. "Can he travel, will he survive the move, how long will he be gone, will we need to make preparations for his departure!?"

"Your majesty, please give me a chance to address your concerns as we prepare the King for the journey. We can leave in the morning, the earlier the better. But, in the morning, it will be very important that we waste no time and move him as quickly and safely as possible." Dr. Ross stated calmly as he tried to lessen the Queen's fears.

"I will think on it." The Queen walked back and forth across the floor as she gathered her wits about her. "You will need one additional person who will be most important on this trip and that is a seeker. We have three in the kingdom, but Gretchen will be the best to guide you since she knows your world very well. Then, I must ask that Prince James accompany you, too. Prince John must remain since he is the rightful heir to the throne. We will hope that all goes well and the King will return to us in good health. What will you need and how will we get the King to the portal?" The Queen now looked to Dr. Ross for guidance.

"Ok, we will need to be able to transport him as quickly as possible but as smoothly as possible.

Do you have any carriages or other means of transportation that would fit that description?"

"I do have one idea that may work for that purpose. Adelaide, will you please tell Cedric to summon Arius and tell them both to hurry. It is important."

"Aye, your majesty!" And Adelaide rushed out the door and down the hall.

Within minutes, a man appeared out of nowhere and stood next to the queen. "I am here, your majesty. May I be of some service." And he bowed to the queen.

"Where did he come from?" Dr. Ross blurted out.

"Oh, Arius, you have arrived! Dr. Ross, this is Arius. He is our wizard. Arius, we need your help! The King is ill and needs to go through the portal to have surgery. Dr. Ross says he needs to take the King to someplace called a "hospital". It is his heart and Dr. Ross is here to help heal him. We need you to transport four people to the portal at first light: The King, Dr. Ross, Prince James, and Gretchen."

"I would prefer that to be five people," Dr. Ross added. "I would like Justine go with us, too. That way it isn't just me. We were visiting Stonehenge as a family and it would be better if a family member was with me. Then we could pretend an emergency arose while on the tour and she needed to remain with me. And, of the four in my family, she is the only one who can see and hear Gretchen."

"So be it, then five people, please. Adelaide, please go gather Justine and Prince James and tell them that they will be traveling very early in the morning and tell Gretchen, too. And please hurry!" Adelaide left the room very quickly to locate the three remaining travelers.

She found Gretchen still waiting outside the palace door and informed her that the Queen needed her presence immediately and that Gretchen was to accompany her to the King's chamber. When they reentered the palace, Adelaide saw Justine and Prince James climbing the stairs having just completed the tour. She yelled for them to stop and explained the situation to all three. Then they all ran the rest of the way up the stairway, down the hall, and into the bedchamber.

"Dad, what's going on? Are we going back through the portal?" Justine inquired out of breath.

"Mother, I do not understand! I thought father was doing better!"

"I am sorry, James, but there is no time to explain right now. We need to move the King to the portal at first light. And that is where Arius will be most helpful. Arius will be able to use his powers to transport everyone to the portal with one of his spells. It is important that Gretchen stay with the group, no more than a mile away from anyone the whole time you are gone. Gretchen, you will need to help Dr. Ross get where he needs to go and then stay with the group, invisible at all times, until you are needed to bring them back to Wiltshire. Please promise me that you will follow these instructions."

"We promise," they all said together.

"I'll be able to communicate with Gretchen since I already have this necklace and will be able to see and hear her." Justine threw in. "I'll make sure no one gets lost!"

"We need to get the King ready to travel. He will need to be as inconspicuous as possible." Dr. Ross added.

"I can help with that," Arius stated confidently. "I can change his appearance and place him in a deep sleep so he is comfortable during the journey."

"But will he awaken at some point? I want to be able to do the surgery without any magic spells interfering with it." Dr. Ross liked the idea that the King would be able to travel without incident, but was concerned that the spell might wear off and the King could wake up in the middle of surgery.

"Not to worry. Gretchen has enough magic to wake him when needed." Then Arius said a chant and moved his arms in front of him from side to side. The King was now wearing new clothes and appeared to be in a deep sleep.

"I, as well, will need to wear clothes suitable for the journey, Arius." Prince James insisted.

"Very well, young Prince." So, Arius said a chant, waved his arms, and James now looked presentable for the trip. In fact, his outfit looked just like the one Luke had on.

"Thank you, Arius." James said as he checked out his new clothes.

Dr. Ross examined the group of travelers and was pleased with the way everything was coming together. "The King should travel very well now. He is resting comfortably. I don't think any of us will arouse suspicion once we pass through the portal. Queen Marianne, will you please tell my wife and Luke where we have gone and that we will return as soon as King William is stable. I told her I wouldn't leave her behind as long as we are here, but this can't be helped. I hope she'll understand and forgive me."

"Aye, I will let them know you have left," the Queen replied.

The group of travelers prepared overnight for the journey. And just before the sun came up, the King was placed on a stretcher so he would travel comfortably during the trip. Then all five stood together in the middle of the room. Dr. Ross and Prince James were holding the stretcher and Gretchen and Justine needed to place their hands on the stretcher as well so they would all travel together. Arius began to say some words that sounded similar to what Gretchen said when the family had originally gone through the portal. Then suddenly, they were gone.

# CHAPTER 17

## THE TRIP BACK TO THE FUTURE

The five travelers, a little dizzy from their short journey, saw that they were standing in front of the portal that was going to take them back to the future. Dr. Ross looked around to make sure everyone had made it in one piece and checked on the King.

"I think we're ready to go through the portal, Gretchen." Dr. Ross motioned to Gretchen to start.

"I must tell you that each one of you will be invisible once you go through the portal. That will ensure the existence of the portal remains a secret. But you will be able to see each other."

Gretchen began a chant to open the portal and motioned to the group to go through it. One by one, they entered the portal and appeared on the other side of the massive stone that was part of Stonehenge. Dr. Ross and Justine were now back in familiar surroundings.

There was no time to lose, and Dr. Ross started to devise a plan. As he looked around, he noticed there were only four of the five travelers who had come through the portal. Alarmed, he asked, "Where's Gretchen?"

"Dad, she's here! But right now, I guess I'm the only one who can see or hear her," Justine replied.

"She just told me you will be able to communicate with her if you need to but you won't be able to see or hear her."

"Ok, as long as we know where she is. It looks like the tour group is still in the same place it was when we left! Dr. Lange was right! The Portal has taken us back to the exact moment when we left! Gretchen, are we visible yet?"

"She says that once we move out away from the portal, we will be visible again."

Dr. Ross left the group and approached the tour guide. "Excuse me sir, Rob is it? I'm a doctor and one of our tour group seems to have taken seriously ill. It's important that we call for an ambulance and get him to a hospital."

Justine ran over to her dad's side and whispered, "Dad, Gretchen says that the best hospital is in Oxford which is nearby."

"And I would prefer the ambulance come from the hospital in Oxford, please."

"What?" Replied the startled tour guide. "Which one of the tourists is sick?"

"That's not important now, what is important is that we get him the help he needs right away!"

"Yes sir, I'll call for that ambulance immediately!"

"Thank you. I'll be over there attending to the patient." Dr. Ross and Justine walked back over to be with Prince James and the King. "Prince James, I think it best if we just call you James while we're here. We don't want to arouse suspicion and call attention to your father. We also need to refer to him as William ... by the way, I don't think anyone ever told us your last name."

"Aye, it is Pendragon. And I understand why it is important to use my first name."

"Pendragon? Wasn't that the last name of the legendary King Arthur?" Dr. Ross asked.

"Aye, he was one of our ancestors. I understand that the history of your England is very different than the England I live in, as Dr. Lange has told us many times. Ours, it seems, has taken a different path!" James said. "And I am surprised at how different this Stonehenge looks than the one in my kingdom. It is very much old and worn down!"

Just then they heard the sirens coming from a distance. "What is that awful noise?" James bellowed.

"That's the noise the siren makes on the ambulance. The siren warns people to get out of the way when it's traveling on the roads. It's coming to take the King, I mean, your dad to the hospital." Justine informed him.

"That is very loud and hurts my ears," James added. "And what is that awful beast moving very fast towards us?" he blurted out. "I will protect you! Get behind me." James grabbed Justine's arm and pulled her behind him. Then he went for his sword but nothing was there.

"Thank you for trying to protect me, but that "beast" won't hurt us. That's the ambulance, I mean, it's a carriage run by a motor that helps to transport sick people to the hospital."

"Ah, I understand the word 'motor' since we have those in Wiltshire now."

The ambulance pulled up and the paramedics got out and approached Dr. Ross. "Are you the doctor in need of an ambulance?"

"Yes, I'm Dr. Ross. I'm a heart surgeon from the United States. This person needs to get to the hospital ASAP and he may need surgery. You need to start an antibiotic IV immediately."

The paramedics carefully transferred the King from the stretcher to the ambulance bed, began an IV, and checked his vital signs.

"He seems to be unresponsive, in some kind of deep sleep," said one of the paramedics.

"He's okay. I needed to give him something to make it safe for him to travel here," Dr. Ross answered.

"Travel? I'm confused," the other paramedic chimed in. "I thought he was one of the tourists from the group over there."

"He is! I just meant to travel in the ambulance so he would be more comfortable, to keep him stable." Dr. Ross knew he had almost blown it.

"You're the doctor." The paramedics loaded the King into the ambulance. "We're ready to go, Dr. Ross."

"These two young people need to go with the ambulance, too. This is his son and my daughter."

"Okay, please get in the back and we'll get you to the hospital as quickly as possible."

So, Dr. Ross, Justine, James, and Gretchen got into the back of the ambulance. The paramedic closed the doors and the ambulance sped off to the hospital.

# CHAPTER 18

## THE QUEEN EXPLAINS

"Mother, where is everyone? How is father doing? I haven't seen Dr. Ross this morning. And now that I think about it, I didn't see Gretchen at the front door, either." Prince John had just located his mother in the main hallway and he was followed by Luke and the princesses.

"John, I have a lot to tell you but we must find Mrs. Ross so everyone will hear what I say at the same time." Queen Marianne rang the bell and Cedric entered the hall. "Cedric, please go gather Mrs. Ross and bring her to the Great Hall. We will all be waiting for her there."

Cedric went to the bedchamber that had been assigned to Mrs. Ross and knocked on the door. "Coming, just a minute." She threw on some clothes and opened the door. Cedric relayed that she was needed in the Great Hall as soon as possible. She grabbed her shoes and followed him to where both families were waiting.

"It is indeed good that you are present, Mrs. Ross. There are many things I need to tell all of you."

"All of us? I don't see my husband anywhere..." Mrs. Ross began and she was interrupted by the Queen.

"Mrs. Ross, it is very important I tell you everything that has happened and I hope it will be clear when I am done."

So, the Queen began by telling them the King's condition had become worse late last night and he had trouble breathing. She told them that Dr. Ross decided the only way to help him was to take the King through the portal to a hospital because the King may be in need of surgery.

"Surgery? Back through the portal? You mean father is not here? When will he return? What does that mean for the kingdom of Wiltshire right now? Who will be making decisions?" John was visibly worried about his father and the kingdom.

"My husband is currently back in our time period and he didn't tell me he was leaving!" Now, Mrs. Ross was also upset because she had been left alone again after Drew had just promised he wouldn't leave her. At home, she didn't mind as much when he was gone for long periods of time because she had many projects to help keep her busy. But this was different! Now, she was in a strange country and not even in the 21$^{st}$ century at that! This just made things worse!

"I will answer all your questions in time, but please, we need to continue to act like the King is still here and resting in his bedchamber. We must tell the people of Wiltshire that he is being attended to by Dr. Lange and Dr. Ross and we will inform them if anything changes." The Queen stated trying to calm Prince John and Mrs. Ross.

"Mom, we'll be okay," Luke said as he hugged his mother. "Prince John has introduced me to his kingdom and I think we'll be fine until Dad returns. Please don't worry. Besides, you've still got me!"

As she looked around the room, Mrs. Ross realized that Justine wasn't part of the group. "Where is Justine?" she shouted. "I don't see her! What has happened to my daughter?"

"Mrs. Ross, nothing has befallen her. She is with your husband and so is Prince James. It was Dr. Ross who asked that Justine go with him. He thought it best to have a family member with him and also, Justine is the only one who can see and hear Gretchen. I asked that James go as well in order to help with William. John had to remain since he is to succeed William if anything happens. I am praying that my husband is returned to us healed and everything will be as it was."

"I am speechless," Stephanie said with a sigh. "I could never have dreamed up a situation like this if I tried! Luke, I think it's important that you and I stay together until your dad returns. Or at least stay close."

"As long as I'm with John, I think I'll be okay, Mom. Please don't worry about me right now. I think we should concentrate on Dad and Justine and hope that everyone comes back safely."

"I think we should all take a moment to relax and sit down to breakfast," and the Queen motioned to everyone to have a seat at the table.

"I'm not very hungry," Mrs. Ross whispered to Luke. "I'm too worried to be hungry."

"Mom, you need to eat. We haven't really had a meal since we got here. We need to make sure we take care of ourselves while Dad and Justine are gone," Luke said trying to reassure his mom as they followed the Queen to the table. "And besides, look at all that food! We can't let that go to waste!"

Everyone sat down and Cedric started serving. There wasn't much conversation during breakfast. It seemed like everyone was worried about the travelers. But Luke hadn't lost his appetite. He asked for seconds of almost everything. Finally, Prince John broke the silence.

"Mother, what are we to do while father is away. Who will make the decisions regarding the kingdom right now? What if one of the other kings gets word that father is sick?"

"I am so sorry this had to happen and that we are facing this problem right now. This all happened so quickly and there was no time to let you know that your father was leaving. Prince John, you will be making decisions in your father's sted until he returns."

"Me? I am not prepared to run the kingdom!" John interrupted.

"Aye, you are. Your father has taught you much and he has included you in many of the decisions he has made regarding the people of this kingdom. You have also learned much about our kingdom and about the past. I know you will be able to reach deep into what you have learned and do your very best." Then the Queen put her hand on his arm, "You are your father's son and will be just and fair when making a decision. You will be a great king someday!"

"Thank you, Mother. I will do as you wish."

And not to be outdone, both princesses chimed in at the same time, "What can we do, Mother? We are good at making decisions, too!"

"Perhaps, we could decide what to eat for our meals, or whether we need to do our lessons each day." Princess Bethany said with assurance and smiled at the Queen.

"Thank you for your help, girls, but I think I can still make the decisions for you children! Right now, I think it important we remain calm and continue following our day-to-day schedule and get ready to start a new day."

"Yes, Mother," Madison said in agreement.

"Do we have to keep on schedule, Mother? I do not want to do lessons." Bethany chimed in.

"Come, Bethany. Let us go upstairs and start the day like Mother asked," and Madison motioned to Bethany to leave the table.

"I will do as Mother has asked," Bethany had resigned herself to the fact that she couldn't convince her mother to let them skip their lessons even for just one day.

And with that, everyone left the table to retreat to their bedrooms.

# CHAPTER 19

## REGISTRATION

The paramedics stayed in contact with the hospital during the trip there. They had alerted the hospital staff that Dr. Ross was with them and would be the attending physician. Once the ambulance arrived, Dr. Ross began instructing those who met them at the door. He ordered some tests to be run immediately and scheduled a surgery room. The King was lifted out of the ambulance and transported into the hospital followed by James, Justine, and the invisible Gretchen. The staff immediately began attending to the patient per Dr. Ross' instructions. The trip had been a lot longer than Dr. Ross had hoped and knew that time was of the essence or he might lose his patient.

"We need to register your patient so I need to ask you some questions, please," said the registration attendant who was following them.

"James and Justine, will you please go with this lady and answer any questions she has regarding the K..., I mean, William?"

"Yes, we can, but what do we say when she asks about insurance and how he will pay for his stay?" Justine asked.

"Just tell them that I will cover all costs for this patient." Dr. Ross informed her.

"Okay, if you say so! Come on, James, we need to go with this nice lady.

"I will stay with the King," Justine heard Gretchen say. "Since you have the necklace, I will be able to communicate with you anywhere in the hospital."

So, they followed the lady down the hall to register the King.

She led them to a cubicle where she had her computer set up for registration. "This is very unusual for me to take information from a minor, but in this instance, we will make an exception."

"Where are we, what are we doing here, who is she, and what is that thing in front of her?" James asked politely but firmly. Justine gently kicked his foot under the table. "Ow, what was that for?"

"Just let me handle this. I'll explain everything later." Justine was hoping he would stop asking questions.

The receptionist looked puzzled not knowing what to make of these two.

"It's okay, he doesn't get out much," Justine tried to brush off the questions and get on with the registration.

"Okay, right then. What is the name of the patient?"

"William Pendragon," Justine said.

"William what? Did you say Pendragon? Are you kids pulling my leg?"

"No, we are not pulling your leg nor any other part of your body," James replied surprised.

"Oh, that's just an expression, James. She didn't actually mean ... oh never mind. No, we are very serious, that's his name. And he is 40 years old, right James?"

"Aye, that he is."

"I hope you two are being truthful right now," the lady stated accusingly.

"Oh, we are, believe me, you don't know the half of it!" Justine said under her breath.

"What was that?"

"Oh nothing, please ask your questions so we can go check on his father."

The lady finally got to the last question regarding payment. "Final question, who or what insurance should I list as the responsible party for this hospital visit?"

"We are not having a party. We are here so that my father will get the help he needs," James replied. And again, Justine kicked his foot. "What, what did I say?"

"Please, excuse him, he's worried about his dad, which is understandable. Now, to answer your question, my dad, Dr. Ross, said he will cover the cost of this hospital stay, whatever that may be."

"Do you need help to pay for my father?" And then James pulled out some gold coins from a satchel he was carrying under his shirt. Once Justine saw what he was holding, she immediately grabbed his hand and made him put the coins back in the bag. "What are you doing? I thought you needed some coins."

"Not really, please don't worry about it right now. We can settle this later." Justine quickly added. "Are we done yet? We really need to go see how his father is doing?"

"Yes, I think we're done. This has been most unusual and I hope he will be okay," the receptionist said to Justine as she motioned toward James.

"Oh, yes! I think he'll be fine. Now would you please direct us to the floor where we need to go to find his father? I think he's really worried!"

The receptionist told them to go to the 5th floor since the King was being prepared for surgery.

As they were leaving, James looked at Justine, "What were you doing? You kicked me two times! And why could I not use the coins in my bag? I picked them up before we left."

"I kicked you because you were asking too many questions! I know why you were, but don't ask any more in front of these people, please? They won't understand why you don't know anything. Well, I mean, what I mean is, you have no idea what is going on in 2020, so please let me explain it to you when no one is listening. And as to the money, no one carries around gold coins in the 21$^{st}$ century."

"I am sorry. I did not think about that. I will be more careful. But you will need to remember that this is all new to me."

"Agreed. Now, I need to talk to Gretchen. Gretchen, are you there?"

"I'm here. Are you two done with your task?"

"Yes, is everything okay? How is the King? James is worried about his father."

"Yes, for right now, to answer your first question. Your father is getting ready to move the King into surgery. I will remain with the King and watch over him."

"Okay, we're on our way to the fifth floor right now." Then speaking to James, "Your father is going into surgery right now. Gretchen didn't say why but I'm sure we'll find out later. Don't worry about your dad. I know he's in good hands. My father is a fantastic heart surgeon."

"Thank you for your kind words. How long do you think this surgery will be?"

"I don't know yet, but we might be able to find out when we get to the fifth floor. Oh my gosh, speaking of the fifth floor, we have to go up the elevator to get there! That will be an experience! Just follow me and don't act too surprised when we do this."

"Do what, exactly?"

"You'll see, follow me."

# CHAPTER 20

## SURGERY AND RECOVERY

So, Justine took James to the elevator and pushed the up button. When the door slid open, James let out a gasp and then immediately acted like he had to cough. He followed Justine onto the elevator and had to steady himself when it started to move. It was a glass elevator, and James could see the ground disappear as the elevator climbed to the fifth floor. He started to laugh, "I have never seen anything like this! We are going up! How does this work? Will it go faster? What is this that allows me to see out of it?" as he points to the window.

"Boy, it's a good thing no one else is on the elevator! The thing that allows you to see through it is called glass and makes a window. And..."

"We must get one of these for my kingdom!" James said excitedly!

"I don't think you'd be able to get all the equipment needed to make one through the portal!" Justine replied.

"You are right, of course! I would love to have one in the palace. I guess if I want to ride in one then I will have to go through the portal more often!"

The doors opened to the lobby of the fifth floor and the two approached the nurse's station. "His father is in surgery right now and Dr. Ross is his surgeon. Can you tell us how the surgery is going or how much longer it might be, please?" Justine inquired of the nurses.

"Let me see, oh yes, he's still in surgery and may be there for a while. I'm sorry, but I don't have any more information to share with you right now." The nurse informed them. "You can sit in the waiting area over there, to your left. We will let you know if we hear anything."

"Thank you. Do you know where we could get something to eat?" Justine asked. They hadn't eaten anything since they left Wiltshire and she was very hungry.

"Yes, there are vending machines in the waiting area and there is a cafeteria on level 0."

"Thank you again. James, we need to go over there to wait." The two of them sat down in the waiting area away from other people so they could talk. "I need to contact Gretchen to see how the surgery is going. Just act like I'm talking to you so it doesn't look like I'm talking to myself."

"Aye," James replied. So, James started moving his mouth like he was talking to Justine.

"Gretchen, can you hear me?"

"Yes, Justine, I hear you. Where are you and James right now?"

"We're sitting in the waiting area on the same floor you're on. How is the surgery going? Is the King still okay?"

"Yes, I had to wake him from his sleep so another doctor could come in and make him go back to sleep. That seemed very strange to me, but I did it. There is a machine in this room that continues to beep and I have surmised that I am hearing his majesty's heartbeat. It changes every now and then, but your father doesn't seem concerned at this point."

"That's very good news. I'll let James know. How much longer do you think the surgery will be?"

"I heard your father say they needed to fix a valve and then close up. As to how long, I think I heard him say it would depend on how smoothly the surgery goes."

"Well, James and I are pretty hungry so I think we'll get something to eat. Let us know when my dad is done."

"I will do that. I will keep you informed of their progress."

"James, Gretchen said your father is doing very well. My dad is repairing a valve in his heart but Gretchen wasn't sure when the surgery might be over. I'm sure we'll have time to go get something to eat. I'm starved!"

"I am glad father is doing well. What do you mean when you said that your dad is repairing a valve?"

"Oh, wow! I keep forgetting you don't have the same information in 1520 that we have now. Just keep asking questions if you don't know something. I can only tell you what I know. Valves are part of the heart and they open and close to let blood and oxygen flow through the heart to the rest of the body. Sometimes they don't work right. That must be what my dad is replacing. He can tell you more when he's done. Ok, now can we get something to eat?"

"I am most hungry! I need to eat very soon." James replied.

"Well, follow me. I don't know what the food line has in it today, but we will soon find out."

"Food line?"

"Good grief, let's just get there and I'll show you!" And Justine grabbed his hand to lead him to the elevator. When she realized what she had done, she immediately dropped his hand and looked away. "Oh, I'm so sorry! I didn't mean to do that!"

"You may hold my hand if you wish, I rather like it!" James admitted. Then he took her hand as they got on the elevator and a huge smile spread across her face.

On the way down, Justine explained to him that they were going to a cafeteria and would be able to pick the food items they wanted. She told him he needed to listen to her and not to act very surprised by what he would see. He agreed.

They arrived on level 0. As the door opened, they could smell the aroma of food wafting through the air. They turned the corner and the cafeteria came into view. Immediately, James' eyes grew very large. He had never seen so much food in one place! He was having trouble containing himself. Just as he was about to speak, Justine grabbed his hand to help steady him and they walked together into the cafeteria. Justine showed him his lunch choices and then the desserts.

"I think I want it all!" James exclaimed. "How do you decide after seeing all of these choices?"

"I just pick what looks good at the time, and what I feel like eating. But I've had many of these foods and know what probably tastes good. I can help you pick if you like."

"That would be most helpful, thank you."

Justine led him down the line and helped him pick foods she thought he would like. When they got to the desserts, he had trouble picking one, but finally decided on chocolate cake. They took the trays to the cashier and Justine took out a credit card to pay for their dinners.

"What is that?" James asked.

"Oh, that's a credit card," she answered. "We can use it instead of money."

"Hasn't he ever heard of a credit card?" the cashier asked.

"He's from out of town!" Justine shrugged. Then she put the card into the chip reader.

"That thing is eating your card!" James yelled and tried to grab the card as it went into the machine.

"It's okay, James! Please don't touch it. Oh, rats! Now we have to start over since you interrupted the reader." And Justine started the transaction again and this time with no disruptions.

Justine found a table in the corner of the room, away from everyone, to eat their "late" lunch. James was pleasantly surprised at how good everything tasted. He asked a lot of questions during lunch about the cafeteria, who cooked the food, why do so many people eat there, how did the credit card work. His head was spinning with all the things he had encountered in such a short time. Justine had a hard time trying to keep up with all the questions he had.

They had just finished lunch when Justine heard Gretchen's voice. She told Justine that the surgery was finished and was a success. Justine exclaimed, "Yes!" rather loudly and attracted the attention of all those at tables around them. She told James the good news and informed Gretchen they had just finished eating and would be right up.

"May I push the button this time?" James asked as they approached the elevator.

"Sure, go ahead!"

When they got off on the fifth floor, Dr. Ross was there to greet them.

Justine gave her dad a big hug. "Oh, Dad! I'm so proud of you! Gretchen told me the surgery was a success."

"Yes, it was. Now we're just waiting for him to wake up. He's in recovery right now."

"Recovery, what is that?" James asked.

"I'm sorry, James. I think I need to explain everything that has happened up to this point." They sat down in the waiting room and Dr. Ross explained what was wrong with his father's heart, described the surgery, and why he was currently in recovery. James thanked him for all he had done to heal his father for he felt that without Dr. Ross having made the decision to leave Wiltshire, his father would not have survived.

# CHAPTER 21

## THE PLAN FOR THE DAY

"If you are to walk around in Wiltshire, you need different clothes. Everyone will stare at you!" John stated as he pulled some clothes out of James' wardrobe. "However, the people will know you are a stranger since everyone knows everyone here."

"Great! I think it'll be so cool to be able to look like you, a person from the past! You've put out several things. Where do I start?" Luke asked since he wasn't sure what to put on first.

John showed him how the layers of clothing went on and Luke proceeded to get dressed. Then they went down the stairs to the Great Hall to have lunch.

"Hey, Mom, how do I look?" And Luke showed her what he was wearing. "Now I look like one of the natives. I can mingle and the people won't even notice me!"

"You look like you belong here. But I hope you're not planning to go anywhere outside the castle, are you, Luke?" Mrs. Ross certainly didn't want to lose track of the only family member with her.

"No, of course not. Why would I? I know better than that, especially right now."

"Good. I was worried because it sounded as if you were going 'sight-seeing'." Mrs. Ross knew her son and if he had the opportunity to venture out into a "new" place he wouldn't hesitate.

"He would not be able to leave the palace without us knowing it," the Queen assured her. "We have guards at each door to the palace and on the castle walls. They will tell us if he is seen outside the palace."

"Great, because I'm staying right here. There's so much to do within these walls! Why would I want to leave?" Luke said sarcastically. "I don't want to check out the street markets, and walk, and check out the street markets ..."

"He can be with us," Bethany and Madison chimed in.

Then Madison added, "We can show him the games we play, how to needlepoint, play the piano...Oh, mother, can we take him riding? Please, oh please! That would be so much fun. John could come with us!"

"I do not think that to be a good idea with your father gone right now."

"Oh, please. We will take great care and not go very far. Just to the top of the hill and back?" Bethany asked.

"The hill is rather far away and outside the castle walls. It would take you most of the afternoon to ride that distance." The Queen said thoughtfully. "And I certainly wouldn't want you to travel any farther than that."

"That does sound pretty cool," Luke admitted. "I would love to ride a horse."

"You've never ridden a horse in your life!" Mrs. Ross replied. "You'll probably fall off!"

"Not if I ride a gentle one!" Luke assured her.

"I will go with them, mother, and make sure everyone remains safe." Prince John told the Queen.

"No, John, you need to remain here. Your father is not in the kingdom and you must be here. I think this would be a good task for Arius today."

"Then we can go, Mother?" Madison pleaded.

"Aye, if Arius will be with you three. But only if he goes! And you will do whatever he tells you to do. Remember, only to the top of the hill."

"Who is Arius?" Luke asked.

"I am sorry. I forgot you two have not met. He is our sorcerer," the Queen said matter-of-factly.

"Sorcerer! You have a sorcerer? Mom, did you hear that! They have a sorcerer!"

"Yes, Luke. I heard her. This sorcerer is reliable, right? Can he be counted on to take care of my son?"

"You have no need to worry, Mrs. Ross. The children will be well looked after," the Queen announced.

"We can show Luke more of the kingdom!" the girls said excitedly.

"I will talk to Arius and let him know what we have decided. As you wait, you girls need to eat your lunch and the stable boys will attend to the horses."

"Thank you, Mother," Madison stated very courteously.

"Ok, Mom, they have permission from the Queen, now do I have your permission to go and with a sorcerer no less?" Luke queried.

After a moment's reflection, she agreed that he could go. "But you can't take any chances, Luke. Promise me."

"I'll be very careful, Mom. Scout's honor!" And Luke proceeded to finish his lunch looking forward to trying something new.

# CHAPTER 22

## WHERE'S LUKE?

As soon as they had all finished eating, Bethany and Madison almost pulled Luke to the stables. When they arrived, they found the horses ready to go. Luke looked around and noticed the stable area was very clean. Surrounding the cobblestone courtyard where they were standing were many stalls of horses, their heads hanging over the doors munching on hay.

"Where is Arius?" Bethany was anxious to get going and started looking around for the 'babysitter'.

"I cannot believe I have to do this," Arius said as he appeared before them. "The Queen thinks this is a good idea. Well, I do not! I am a wizard, not someone who is a caretaker for children!"

"Mother said no riding unless someone is with us and you are the one!" Madison asserted. "John has to stay within the castle walls so that leaves you. Be happy, Arius! This will be fun!"

"Riding horses is not my idea of fun. Especially when I go wherever I want without one!" Arius looked perturbed by the whole thing. But he was going to do it because the Queen asked him to, and he wasn't going to disobey her. Besides, it was his job to keep the royal family safe. "You must be Luke. Nice to meet you."

"And you are a real sorcerer! I've never met one before. I didn't think they existed outside of storybooks."

"Well, they do, I do. And please, don't ask me to do any magic tricks! Now, find your horse so we can get this thing over with."

"Here is the horse for you, Luke. Her name is Ruffles and she is gentle and easy to ride. She is my horse but I want you to ride her today. You will not have any trouble with her."

Madison handed Luke the reins and they all walked the horses out of the stable area into a small grassy spot. The princesses gave Luke some preliminary instructions on how to ride a horse since he had never ridden before, the two most important being how to stay on and stop.

All four riders climbed up on the horses and settled into their saddles. Bethany and Madison were riding side saddle which was the proper way for a girl to sit a horse. Gathering the reins, they all started to walk toward the castle gates.

"This is so awesome!" Luke yelled and almost spooked the horse with his excitement. "Wow, I didn't know Ruffles could be so sensitive to noises. Good thing she's the gentle one. I'll try not to yell from now on."

"This is supposed to be an uneventful trip to the top of the hill and then back again. Please be careful. I do not want to go back to the castle with an injured child." Arius glanced at Luke with a disgruntled look. He wasn't happy to be there in the first place. He definitely didn't want anything to happen on his watch.

The guards turned the large wheel that raised the castle gates and then lowered the drawbridge to allow the small band of riders to exit the safety of the castle walls. The princesses clicked and their horses started trotting forward across the drawbridge. Of course, Luke's horse followed and Luke started bouncing all over the place. He grabbed the pommel of the saddle to help steady himself because he was finding it difficult to stay on. He didn't want to fall off! How would that look in front of the princesses? Arius took up the rear so he could keep an eye on them. Once outside the castle, Luke noticed how green and rolling the countryside was. He hadn't noticed that when they arrived. The grass was knee high on the horses and swayed back and forth in the breeze as the horses made their way toward the hill. He put his hand out and could almost touch the grass. There were trees along the periphery of the fields, but none in front of them. All that lay in front of them were grass fields.

The girls located a beaten down path near them and began to follow it up the hill. Luke looked ahead of him and realized the "hill" was more like a small mountain. As they began their ascent, Luke noticed some deer grazing in the distance. As soon as the deer saw the intruders, they darted off into the trees. Parts of the climb were somewhat steep and Luke saw the girls lean forward in their saddles so he did the same. Luke turned around to look behind him and saw the castle getting smaller and smaller. This was a much farther ride than he had anticipated. But the countryside was beautiful and he got lost in the scenery. He wasn't paying attention to the riders in front of him and Ruffles almost ran into Bethany's horse. Once he realized how close he was, it was too late!

"Luke, watch where you're going!" Bethany exclaimed. "You almost made me fall off!"

"I'm sorry, Princess Bethany. I was paying more attention to the scenery and not watching where I was going!" Luke apologized for being so careless. "It's so green here! I'm so used to being in the cement jungle!"

"Cement what?" Bethany said confused.

"I forgot. You don't have roads like we do. This is like being out in the country at home, out in farm country.

But we don't go there very often. So, this is a real treat for me!"

They could hear Arius behind them mumbling to himself. They looked at each other and started laughing.

"What is so funny?" Arius asked.

That made the three of them laugh even harder.

"That is quite enough. Get going. We do not have all day to finish this trip."

And with that, the girls began to canter up the hill. And of course, Ruffles stayed with the other horses since she didn't want to be left behind. This was an easier gait to sit for Luke and he found himself enjoying going faster.

"Now this is more like it! Race you to the top!" He yelled. And he kicked Ruffles really hard and yelled, "Go girl, go!" at the same time. She took off at a gallop and Luke found himself wishing he hadn't done that. He was now hanging on for dear life.

"Luke, pull back on the reins! You need to slow her down!" Arius yelled.

But Luke was so far ahead at that point that he couldn't hear anything. They watched as Luke rode farther and farther away. Then, all of a sudden, Luke disappeared over the top of the hill.

"Arius, Luke just went over the hill! We are never to go over the hill, just to the top!" Madison yelled.

Arius signaled to the girls, "You both ride back to the castle. Go directly there! Do not wait for me. As soon as I find Luke, we will return to the stables." He waited for a moment to make sure the princesses had done what he asked them to do. Then he dismounted, mumbled something and disappeared. His horse took off after the girls and followed them back to the castle.

Luke thought he was going to die. He knew he had crossed over to the other side of the hill which he wasn't supposed to do! He wondered, 'What happens when you go over the hill? Is there a monster ready to pounce on him?' He knew it was a long way back to the castle if he fell off and had to walk. But at the same time, he was having a very hard time trying to stop Ruffles. "Pull on the reins," they said before we left if I want her to stop. For a gentle, easy to ride horse, she sure was ignoring his attempts to stop her.

Just then, Luke felt a hand grab the reins and a familiar voice from behind him. It was Arius! He had suddenly appeared behind him on Ruffles. He let out a huge sigh of relief.

"Boy, am I glad you're here!"

"Pull on the reins as hard as you can! We need to stop this horse before she goes any farther!"

So, the two pulled as hard as they could and Ruffles began to slow her pace to a walk and then finally stopped.

"What were you thinking? Never kick a horse that hard then yell!" Arius scolded Luke. "You went over the hill when you were only to go to the top! We are now in another kingdom and they do not like it when people just drop in on them!"

"I'm sorry. I thought it would be fun to race the girls to the top of the hill but I guess I got carried away!"

"Carried away is correct! Now let us return to the castle before anyone sees us! This will be most inappropriate, but I guess the horse will have to come with us!" Then Arius said some strange words and the three vanished. The next thing Luke knew, they were back in front of the stables within the castle walls.

"Wow! What just happened? One minute we were sitting on Ruffles on the other side of that hill way over there and the next minute, we're still sitting on the same horse but here, in the castle, in front of the stables where we started! Can you teach me how to do that?" Luke thought if he could learn **this** trick, he could really impress his friends at home.

"We need not worry about that now. Most important is to be sure the princesses made it back to the castle and then try to explain all of this to the Queen! First, we get off the horse." Arius looked around to see if the princesses' horses were in the stable area. He didn't see them so told Luke he would be right back. He reappeared and said, "I just saw the princesses and they are coming through the gate right now. They should be here soon. We will wait for them and then all go to the palace together."

The girls arrived and the stable boys took the horses from them. The princesses had no sooner gotten off their horses when Luke realized they were all standing in the main hall of the palace.

"What a neat way to get where you're going!" as Luke started jumping around with excitement. Then he stopped all of a sudden and put his hand behind him.

"Ow, my butt hurts!"

"First time on a saddle does that to you," Arius smiled and the princesses started laughing. "Now we must go find the rest of the family to let them know we are here."

They didn't have to look very far because Queen Marianne and Mrs. Ross had just entered the hall. As soon as Mrs. Ross saw Luke, she ran over to him, hugged him, and then gave him a love tap on the arm.

"I'm so relieved to see you arrived in one piece!"

"We were so worried!" Madison said and then she looked at Luke and stated, "It is a very good thing you were not hurt! We were afraid for you after you yelled, kicked Ruffles, and she started running toward the top of the hill!"

Then Bethany added, "You did look silly trying to stay on bouncing all over the place!" And they both started laughing.

"I'm glad you two found me so entertaining while I was trying not to fall off!" Luke responded.

"What were you thinking, Luke! You could have been killed riding away on the horse like that!"

"I know, I'm sorry Mom!" Luke apologized. "I wasn't thinking! I got a little overconfident! I thought I was doing a pretty good job up to that point and I thought I could handle her."

"Guess you thought wrong! But I'm glad you're okay." And then she hugged him again.

"Thank you, Arius, for returning him safely to us. I am so glad you went with them," the Queen said gratefully. "Did you run into any trouble? Madison just mentioned that Luke was going toward the top of the hill."

"No, your majesty. He did go over the top of the hill but I think I was able to help him stop the horse before someone saw us. I did not sense anyone in the area."

"That is good to know. I would not want others to know of our guests, why they are here and how they arrived."

"I understand, your majesty, and I hope my actions were swift enough to not call attention to us."

"No one is to leave the castle grounds again. You must all stay within these walls from now on!" the Queen ordered.

"Yes, your majesty, I understand," Luke stated humbly. He knew his actions could have put the kingdom in danger and he was truly sorry.

"And that means you both as well, Madison and Bethany. No sneaking out when no one is looking!"

"We understand, Mother. No sneaking out, just stay within the castle walls," they both replied regretfully.

"Good, I am glad everyone agrees. Now please go wash so we may sit down for dinner."

# CHAPTER 23

## THE KING AWAKENS

James and Justine sat in the waiting room hoping for word that the King had awakened from his surgery.

"What are these paper things sitting on this table? Is this some sort of sorcery? Were these people banished into these books?" James asked horrified as he grabbed one of the magazines. There was so much in this new place he didn't understand.

"Those are called magazines. And no, no one is trapped, there was no sorcery involved. Magazines are a way for us to read the news, to find out what's happening around us without actually having to go there."

"Mag a what?"

"They're called magazines." Justine restated. "And no, those aren't actual people, those are pictures. Here, let me show you." Then she took her smartphone out of her pocket, took a picture of James, and showed it to him. "This is called a photo. It makes a picture of you."

"That is of me! This must be magic. So, you take these, what did you call them? Oh, yes, pictures and put them in these things? How do you do this? Why do you do this thing?" he asked. "If we want to know what is happening in the kingdom, we just talk to each other! Whenever anything happens, we all know about it!"

"Well, this isn't a castle where everyone lives within its walls. This talks about a lot of kingdoms all over the place and..."

"Mr. Pendragon is awake now and would very much like to see you." Justine looked up and saw a nurse standing near them.

"Who?" then it dawned on her who the nurse was talking about. "Ohhhh, yes, Mr. Pendragon." Then turning to James, "James, your father is awake and wants to see you."

"Father is awake? I must see him at once!"

"Yes, we must see him at once!" Justine repeated. "Please tell us where we need to go."

"He has been moved from recovery to a private room. I'll take you there. Please, follow me."

Justine and James followed the nurse down the hall to the elevator and up to the tenth floor. James watched out the glass window as the elevator ascended.

"This is not to be believed!" he declared.

"What is?" the nurse asked.

"He just loves to ride in elevators for some reason," Justine threw in.

The doors opened and the nurse took them down the hallway. When they arrived at the room, she motioned to them to open the door.

"He's in there resting. Dr. Ross will join you shortly to explain the patient's follow up. Mr. Pendragon may drop in and out of sleep as he is still groggy from the anesthetic. We have also given him some medicine for the pain."

"Groggy?" James asked.

"I'll explain later," Justine replied as she pushed the door open.

James looked in and saw his father lying on the bed. "Father? Are you awake?" James said hopeful.

"James, is that you?" his father whispered.

"Yes, Father, I am here. It is so good that you are out of surgery. I was worried about you."

"He is doing well."

"Gretchen, is that you?" Justine looked around to see where she was. She saw Gretchen appear near the end of the bed.

"I watched the whole thing. It was very fascinating! When he woke up, he had no idea where he was because when he left the castle, he was still asleep. I have tried to explain the series of events since we left Wiltshire but he does not seem to understood. He is still a little confused."

"Gretchen, are you here, too?" the King inquired in a quiet voice. "Oh, I see you now." Justine realized that she wasn't the only one able to see and hear Gretchen.

"Yes, your majesty. I have been watching over you the whole time."

"Thank you for your loyalty."

"Father, how are you feeling?"

"Very weak, and my chest hurts, but I feel stronger and am breathing better. I am also very tired."

"You are on medicine for the pain and it will make you feel sleepy." Gretchen stated. "That is what I heard Dr. Ross say."

"That I am...sleepy." Then the King drifted off to sleep.

The door opened and in walked Dr. Ross still wearing his scrubs.

"Dad, I'm so glad to see you! And to know that the King is going to be able to go home is wonderful news." Justine said.

"Yes, the surgery was a success, thank goodness. There was a moment when the King's heart stopped but it started right back up again. Now he's on the mend. We just need to make sure he doesn't develop another infection. So, we'll continue to give him antibiotics and pain medicine when needed."

"There is so much to learn in your world! I feel like I am always asking questions!" James interjected.

"Yes, I know!" Justine threw in.

"While the King is sleeping, and Gretchen here to keep and eye on him, I assume she's here."

"Yes, Dad, she's here with us right now. She says she watched the whole surgery."

"Okay, well, I need to talk to James about his dad and what will happen in the coming weeks, here and then back home in Wiltshire. James, will you please follow me out into the hallway?"

"May Justine come to hear as well?"

"Yes, I suppose she can with your permission. I need to talk to family members about decisions that need to be made, and you're it. So, Justine, if you're going to be with us, you need to only offer your opinion if asked. I realize that may be hard for you."

"Hard for me? No, I can be quiet when I need to be." Justine replied. That made her dad laugh.

"Okay. Gretchen, we'll be out in the hallway if you need us for anything."

James and Justine followed Dr. Ross out into the hallway while Gretchen remained with the sleeping King.

# CHAPTER 24

# THE NEIGHBORING KING

"King Henry, sir, one of the castle guards is very anxious to have an audience with you," explained the servant.

"What does he want? Can you not see I am eating my breakfast!" King Henry replied as he continued to gnaw on the meat in his hand.

"Sorry, your majesty, but he insists. He says it is important."

"All right, let him enter." the King said with reservation.

The King was sitting in a large hall eating by himself. The hall had a small fire place located near him and one at the far end. The table was made of oak with very sturdy legs to hold it up. He liked to sit in the middle of the back side of the table because it gave him a good vantage point when anyone would enter the hall. The door opened and in walked one of the castle guards.

"Tell me what is so important you had to interrupt my breakfast!"

"Your majesty, I have just returned to the castle from my security check of the kingdom and saw something that might interest you," the soldier reported.

"What would that be exactly," asked the king as he continued to eat.

"While riding through the kingdom, I saw a rider come galloping over the top of the hill yesterday into our kingdom. But he did not look like he had control of the horse for he kept pulling back on the reins and the horse did not stop. However, that was not the part of most interest. Arius suddenly appeared behind him, I think it to be Arius, the horse stopped, and then all three disappeared."

"That *is* very interesting." King Henry stopped eating and looked up at the soldier. "I wonder why Arius was there. This young man must have been someone of importance otherwise Arius would not have bothered."

"Yes, your majesty, that was my thought, as well. I could not tell who it was on the horse since I was so far away. But both Prince John and Prince James are excellent riders and this young man looked as if he did not know what he was doing. He did, however, have dark hair like them."

"I think we need to visit King William and ask him why someone from his kingdom crossed over into ours." King Henry took one more bite, put the meat bone on the plate and abruptly stood up. "Go and ready a small group of soldiers to accompany me to Wiltshire," he demanded. "I need to know who that boy was, where he came from, and why he appears to be of such importance!"

"Yes, your majesty, at once!" And the soldier left to do the King's bidding.

"What an interesting turn of events! I have suspected something was going on in Wiltshire that they have been hiding from us. Now I have an excuse to find out!" he said to his bodyguard. "Ready my horse, immediately!"

King Henry dressed for the trip, went out of his residence into the surrounding courtyard. A group of ten soldiers were waiting with their horses.

"We are traveling to Wiltshire and will arrive tomorrow. We will camp near the hill tonight and will cross over into Wiltshire in the morning. I am not sure what we will find there, but be on the ready if needed."

"Yes, your majesty." They all chanted together.

King Henry mounted his horse, with assistance, and the small group of travelers exited the castle and left for Wiltshire. They made camp near the edge of the forest at the bottom of the hill on their side that night. So as not to arouse suspicion, they decided it would be best to have a small camp fire since one or two soldiers often camped while making their rounds. Then they cooked the meat they had caught on the road that day.

Because Queen Marianne was worried that someone may have seen Luke and Arius, she had patrols out scouting the kingdom for any sign of intruders. As one of the soldiers traversed the top of the hill, he noticed smoke rising from the trees and decided to investigate. He rode down the hill at a distance toward the trees. He left his horse tied to a tree and then traveled carefully on foot toward the camp. It was very dark, especially under the trees. He suddenly caught his foot on a branch and almost fell but steadied himself just in time. He stopped moving to ascertain if anyone had heard him.

"What was that?" he heard someone say.

"I hear nothing. It was probably an animal. Now eat," was the reply.

"You are probably right. I do not hear it anymore anyway."

Once a few minutes had past, and he was sure no one knew he was there, he proceeded. As he got closer, he heard many voices which seemed strange since only one or two soldiers usually patrolled this area. He crouched down to get a closer look. He could see several silhouettes against the fire, and knew it wasn't just a patrol. He listened carefully to see if he could hear the conversations. Then he heard what he thought was King Henry's voice.

"When we arrive tomorrow, we want this to appear to be a good will visit, nothing out of the ordinary. We must all pay close attention to our surroundings and let me know if you see or hear anything of interest."

The soldier had heard enough and silently but swiftly made his way back to his horse. He mounted in haste and once he was out of ear shot rode as fast as he could. Even though he arrived at Wiltshire late that night, he knew this information couldn't wait. He signaled to the guards on the gate and they lowered the drawbridge. He rode his horse to the palace, jumped off, and knocked on the door several times.

The door finally opened and Cedric inquired as to why he was there at this late hour. The soldier then informed him he had important information for the Queen that couldn't wait. Cedric allowed him entrance to the palace and asked him to remain in the Main Hall. Cedric then went to summon the Queen. The Queen, still in her night gown, appeared covered in a blanket.

"What is it that is so important you felt it your duty to wake me at this time of night?" the Queen asked indignantly.

"I'm sorry your majesty, but I felt it of the utmost importance to tell you now and not wait until morning."

"All right, get on with it."

And the soldier told her what he had seen and heard earlier that night and he projected King Henry would arrive sometime that day. Best guess, he thought it would be in the afternoon.

"I knew this would come to pass! I should never have allowed Madison and Bethany to take Luke on a ride. Especially to the top of the hill. I wish the King was...n't ill! Thank you for this information. I am indeed grateful that you had Cedric wake me. We must take steps at first light to make sure anything that would arouse their suspicion be hidden from view. Please alert the castle guard and the soldiers of this. I will alert the King and give orders at first light. We will follow the plan we have put in place for times such as these."

"Yes, your majesty." Then the soldier bowed and left the palace.

# CHAPTER 25

## THE KINGDOM PREPARES

The sun was just peeking over the horizon when the Queen sent out the alert to everyone to meet in the inner courtyard. A lot of very sleepy citizens arrived not knowing why they were being summoned. The soldiers and the palace guards also circled the area, but they were wide awake and ready to begin. The queen entered the courtyard followed by John, Madison, and Bethany. Mrs. Ross and Luke stood inside the palace and listened.

"Citizens of Wiltshire. I am speaking to you on behalf of the King since he has taken ill and cannot get out of bed at this time. He is being attended to by Dr. Lange and our visitor, Dr. Ross. He has asked me to tell you that King Henry is on his way here right now and should arrive around midday. It is of the utmost importance that we prepare the kingdom for visitors according to our plan and do it with haste. Our kingdom and our way of life will be in grave danger if he or any of his soldiers become aware of what we have here. We have been at peace for ten years now and the King wills it to remain so. Our soldiers will observe to make sure the plan is followed and be able to give orders in the King's stead. Good luck to us all and may God be with us." Then the royal family walked back into the palace.

"Since we are all here, we must check the palace for anything out of the ordinary and put it away. John, you will need to be by my side when King Henry arrives. In no way are we to let on that the King is not here. We must act as if he is in his bedchamber resting. We must not mention Dr. Lange, Dr. Ross, or his family. Mrs. Ross and Luke, you must remain hidden no matter what happens."

"We understand, your majesty. Please tell us where you want us to go and we will be as quiet as a mouse. Sorry, that's just an expression, I mean, no one will know we're here." Mrs. Ross assured the Queen.

"I'm so sorry to have caused all of this!" Luke said apologetically.

"I realize the horse running away with you was something out of your control. But we must put that in the past and deal with the present. Now, everyone, do your part and let us hope this visit goes well."

Right after the Queen had finished addressing the crowd, the people dispersed to all areas within the castle to hide any signs of electrical wires, tools, instruments, bicycles, motors, etc. that had been brought through the portal. The wires became clothes lines, the motors tables, and the other items were placed in camouflaged underground storage areas. The soldiers moved about, checking to make sure things were properly stored and no sign of the "future" existed anywhere within the castle walls.

Around noon, the captain of the guard knocked on the palace door and asked to see the Queen. He informed her that the castle grounds had been checked and rechecked and he was sure all signs of anything from outside the kingdom had disappeared.

"Thank you, Captain. I appreciate all the work that has had to happen this morning. Just to be sure, I will ask Arius to make one final sweep of the area to see if he senses anything that may have been forgotten or is out of place."

"Yes, your majesty. I will also be on the alert while our visitors are here. We will keep our kingdom safe." Then the Captain left the palace to attend to his duties.

The family members had also finished doing a clean sweep of the palace, especially the first floor where the visitors would be. The Queen had asked the family to meet in the Great Hall when done so she would know that their tasks had been completed. Before she met them, she asked Cedric to contact Arius and tell him to meet her there, too. By the time she arrived in the Great Hall, Arius was already there. So were all members of her family plus Mrs. Ross and Luke.

"We have done what you asked, Mother. All evidence of the other world is now gone," John stated confidently. "Mrs. Ross helped me find things that alluded me. She knows the other world much better than I do. We also alerted Dr. Lange regarding the visit. It is good that his office is on the second floor."

"We helped, too!" Madison added not to be outdone. "We took Luke with us and he helped us."

"He was so wonderful," Bethany said adoringly. "He is so strong and was able to lift things we could not."

"Thank you, princesses, but I was just trying to do my part." Luke wanted to help especially since he felt responsible for all of this.

"This is all fine, but your majesty, I am wondering why you summoned me here." Arius would much rather have been somewhere else than listening to all the babbling going on in the room.

"Aye, Arius, I asked you here because I would like you to do a visual sweep in your mind of the kingdom. There must not be anything left behind."

"Yes, your majesty."

Arius closed his eyes and seemed to drift into a trance. He would move his head like he was looking for something, then stop, and then start again. He finally opened his eyes and stared for a minute as if he were trying to wake up. He turned toward the Queen and told her he didn't see or sense anything out of the ordinary and then asked to be excused.

"No, you may not be excused. I need you here with me so I am not always asking someone to look for you. I do not know what will happen when King Henry arrives and we may need your help. You should remain invisible but here by my side."

"Yes, your majesty," and Arius bowed and disappeared.

"Where should Luke and I hide, your majesty? We don't know the palace and am assuming you know of a place that would be hidden from others." Mrs. Ross asked.

"I can show them the hidden passage, Mother, if I may."

"Thank you, John, but I think I will let Madison and Bethany do that."

"We can do that!" Bethany exclaimed.

"I appreciate your willingness to help, Bethany. Thank you. Once you show them where to go, I want you both to remain with them until King Henry leaves."

"Why, Mother? We want to be with you and John. You might need us!" Madison implored.

"I know you want to be with me, and I am grateful. But your safety is more important to me right now. I also would not want one of you to say something related to the ride that we may all regret. So, you both need to stay safely hidden for now."

"I promise we will not talk when they are here." Bethany assured her mother.

"Thank you, but you are ordered to stay put once you are there."

"We would rather be with you, but will stay hidden as you have asked." Madison conceded. "Come on, Bethany, we need to show Mrs. Ross and Luke where we are to hide." Madison took Bethany by the hand and started to walk away. They both looked back at their mother and waved "Good-bye".

Luke and Mrs. Ross followed them up the stairs to hide for the duration of the "visit".

# CHAPTER 26

## THE HOSPITAL STAY

"Your father is healing very nicely, James. He should be able to go home by the end of the week." Dr. Ross said. "I'm very pleased with his progress so far. There's no sign of an infection now and his heart beat is very strong."

"That would be my father, a very strong person inside and out! I was most confident he would be going back to Wiltshire."

During the week, Dr. Ross and Justine had been staying together in a room at the hospital and James stayed in the room with his father. Gretchen continued to remind them that they couldn't be too far away from her at any time. Also, since they only had the clothes on their backs, the hospital staff gave them scrubs to wear and offered to let them use the laundry facility to wash their clothes. Their clothes were beginning to smell after a day or two.

Throughout the week, James and Gretchen kept an eye on the King in between the doctor and nurses' visits. James knew it was his responsibility to ensure his father returned home. James also knew he and his father were both in unchartered territory and he wanted to be around to answer any questions his father had, if he could. He knew his father would be as confused about their surroundings as he was.

When James wasn't with his father, he was with Justine. They often took walks around the hospital but didn't go very far in case James was needed. They felt like they just blended in to their surroundings since they were still wearing their scrubs. During these walks, James learned a lot about how the world had changed since the 1500's. Justine tried to fill him in as much as she could but she had never been interested in history, until now.

On one of their walks, they ran across the Headington Cemetery that had been established in 1885. They found it interesting to walk among the gravestones to see who was buried there, although none of the names meant anything to either one of them. There was a quaint, stone chapel on the grounds which they decided to visit. As they entered, they noticed the beautiful ornate alter at the other end of the chapel. It had been carved out of wood and was surrounded by flowers. On the alter, was a crucifix with a marble likeness of Jesus hanging on a gold cross. They walked in to the center of the chapel and sat in one of the wooden pews. They sat side-by-side and just listened to the silence around them, observing the various statues placed throughout the chapel. James reached over and took Justine's hand. They sat there for a moment staring at the altar. Then James looked over at Justine, reached up with his other hand, turned her head towards his, and gently kissed her. She found herself just melting into the moment. But the moment didn't last very long since they were interrupted by some visitors who had just entered the chapel. Still holding hands, and a little embarrassed, they stood up and decided to leave the chapel.

As they walked hand in hand back to the hospital, they both had the same thought, now what? Just as they arrived at the hospital, it started to pour.

They ran inside, looked at each other and started laughing. Then they both started talking at the same time.

"You mean a lot to me, Justine. I want to be with you."

"I really like you, too, James. I shouldn't have let my guard down. But I can't help it! You're so cute! And I enjoy being with you. I feel like we really connect! I can talk to you!"

"I feel as you do. But we are from two different worlds. Maybe you could stay in Wiltshire while your family goes home."

"I can't leave my family! And besides, I have to finish high school!"

"What is high school?"

"See what I mean?" I don't think this is going to work out."

"Please, give it some more time. We are still going to be together for a while as we need to return to Wiltshire and your father will need to look after the King while he heals. We do not need to decide at this moment." Then Prince James decided to change the topic of discussion. "But for now, you said you were going to show me that computer thing, I think that is what you called it."

"Yes, I was, am. Go see how your father is doing and meet me by the nurse's station in about 30 minutes. I mean, ask Gretchen to contact me and I'll let her know when I'm there."

Justine watched as James walked away knowing that a decision would need to be made sometime in the near future. But for now, she was going to enjoy being with James for as long as she could. She hadn't realized how important he had become to her until that kiss in the chapel.

Justine had been given access to a computer at the hospital and she told James, through Gretchen, where to find her. The computer was located in a little alcove on the tenth floor. The alcove was enclosed by glass walls with an open doorway. James didn't have any trouble finding her.

"This thing called glass is everywhere, is it not? I find it very enjoyable to be able to look outside and this glass does not allow the rain to make us wet! We only have wooden shutters to cover our windows." Then he sat down on a chair near her in front of the computer.

She started the computer. As the screen started to appear, he jumped back off his seat.

"What is that? It must have magical powers like Arius!"

"No, it isn't magic, although at times it does feel like that. Please sit back down. It won't hurt you. It has a hard drive inside it which..." then she saw the look on his face and decided to stop there. "Yep, it has some magic inside it. So...let me show you how it works."

She showed James pictures of places on the earth, one of those being her home state of Indiana. He was amazed at her explanation regarding the actual size of the earth because knowledge of the world during his time was very limited. While she continued to show him pictures and tell him about her life, he just sat there and stared at her in awe.

"Hey, are you paying attention?"

"What, oh, aye. I heard everything you said."

"Okay, just checking."

"I cannot believe how much you know! And I love the way your nose wrinkles while you talk."

"Well, I guess I actually learned something at school! What? My nose wrinkles?"

"Thank you for showing me your home. It is a lot different than living in the palace. This world you live in... so many inventions that make life easier for everyone." Then James looked at Justine and sighed, "I think I have been here too long and need to attend to my father. Please excuse me."

James knew in his head that he shouldn't get involved with Justine, but his heart was a different matter. He wanted to spend as much time with her as he could and hated when he had to leave her. He knew that they were from two different worlds and eventually she would return home. But he would worry about that later and take advantage of all the time they did have together.

He returned to his father's room to assume his duty as Prince and attend to his father. While there, James shared with him all the information he had acquired while being with Justine. So, while his father lay in the hospital bed, James used this time to impart what he learned to educate his father about the world they were in and about the past.

With every day that passed, the King grew stronger and began to gain a ruddy complexion. Along with his strength, he was able to sit up in bed and take walks around the corridors. James was always with him. They had long conversations and his father asked many questions.

"James, I am so impressed with all you have learned during our short time here," his father shared. "I hope to use some of this when we return home. Knowing all of this will make me a better King."

"Father, there is still so much to learn. I will find it hard to leave this world and go back home to ours. Maybe I will be able to return sometime in order to gain more knowledge."

"Unfortunately, I think too much knowledge of this world may be a detriment in our time. There is a danger of being unsatisfied with what is, desiring instead what might be."

"I realize that, Father, but that has already happened and we cannot change that now. Justine told me I can come visit her anytime."

"Justine? I think I understand now. All of this circles back to Justine. My son, you must remember, she will be leaving us at some time. You may be fond of her, but once she leaves, she will become a distant memory, and you will find another young lady in the kingdom that will attract your attention and become your wife."

"Father, I do not want to talk about that now. Yes, I like her, I like her more than you know. She is unlike any young lady in our kingdom. I love being with her. I like talking to her."

Up to that point, both of them had forgotten there was a third person in the room, Gretchen, who felt it was time for her to add a needed piece of information to this scenario.

"Your majesty..." she began.

"Oh, Gretchen! You startled me," the King responded. "I forgot you were in the room!"

"Excuse me, your majesty, but I thought I should interrupt your discussion with a needed bit of information, if I may."

"You may."

"James seems to have forgotten what happens to anyone who visits our kingdom and then returns home. Once someone leaves Wiltshire and goes back through the portal, they lose all memory of the time spent there."

"Yes, I remember." James stated. "But I also know that if they retain possession of the necklace or are accompanied by a seeker, that won't happen. Do we know what happens to someone from our kingdom who travels back and forth other than a seeker? Do we know how far a seeker can go and still retain their powers?"

"Prince James, that has never been done before. I really do not know what might happen to a traveler from our Kingdom!"

"It is not going to happen, James, so there is no need to know that because I will not allow it!" the King stated firmly. "Now, I have to return home as soon as possible to ensure nothing happens to our peaceful kingdom."

"Yes, Father. I understand. I do not like it, but I will abide by what you say." And under his breath he said, "For now."

"Please locate Dr. Ross so we can discuss the journey home," the King commanded. "And please, change into some actual clothes before we leave here."

"I will leave and find him, Father." James knew that tone of voice meant business and he quickly departed the room.

"I think you need to keep and eye on that young man, your majesty. He has a mind of his own."

"That he does, Gretchen, that he does."

# CHAPTER 27

## KING HENRY ARRIVES
## IN WILTSHIRE

Queen Marianne, John, and Arius were anxiously sitting in the Great Hall not knowing when King Henry would arrive. Had they done enough, was the kingdom ready to receive visitors, would they be able to convince him the King was resting in bed? All these thoughts kept going through the Queen's head while they waited. She knew they desperately needed to pull this off in order to keep the peace.

The sound of a distant trumpet stirred her out of her thoughts and she knew the arrival of King Henry was being announced.

"John and Arius, we must prepare ourselves to receive visitors. We will greet them in the courtyard, thank them for visiting our fair kingdom and acknowledge their long journey. We must also inquire as to the reason for their visit. I will invite them into the palace and offer them food and drink to be polite. Then we must encourage them to leave as soon as we feel it is safe."

"Your majesty, what is my role in all of this? Do I really need to be here?" Arius protested.

"Arius, it may be that someone saw you rescue Luke on the hill and I would like you to explain your actions. We, the three of us, must agree, if that is the reason for their visit, on one story to tell. I have given it some thought and this is the one that I think will be fitting. It will be that as you, Arius, were walking through the kingdom, you noticed one of the stable boys mount a horse. You inquired as to the reason and he replied that he was going to exercise the horse and wanted to take it out into the fields for a good run. But things didn't go as planned, and during the run, the horse grabbed the bit and the horse could not be stopped. At that moment, you sensed there was a problem and realized that boy and horse had crossed over the hill. So, you took matters into your own hands and fetched the boy and horse before something happened."

"So that is the story we are to share with the King? Then I now understand why I have been asked to remain with you. I am sorry if that ends up being the reason they are here. I did try to be as discreet as possible when I rescued the lad. But it was rather hard given the circumstances. Your majesty, you had asked that I remain invisible. Am I still to do that?"

"I understand, Arius. And I do not fault you for it. But given the circumstances, I have changed my mind and you are to remain visible for the time being. Now, let us greet our guests as if we have nothing to hide," the Queen announced.

Cedric entered the room and announced that King Henry was in the courtyard accompanied by ten of his royal guard.

The Queen was visibly nervous and John grabbed his mother's arm to help steady her as they walked out the door into the courtyard. There were King Henry and his guard on horseback, a rather impressive sight. As soon as the Queen appeared, King Henry dismounted and his guard followed suit.

King Henry was a short man with a bald head and rather stout. Eating was his favorite way to pass the time in his kingdom. He had only been king for five years since his father died. His father, who had been king before him, had lived for a very long time.

"Greetings, Queen Marianne. It is so good to see you and your son. However, I do not see the rest of the family? I thought they would be here to greet us as well. Might I inquire as to the whereabouts of King William?" King Henry was fishing for information regarding the status of the King.

"It is so good of you to visit our fair kingdom. You must be tired from your journey. As to the family, we do not need to speak of that now. I will inform you of the goings on in the palace once inside. To what do I owe the honor of your visit, sir?"

"We were out hunting game since our kingdom is low on fresh meat. We saw some deer tracks which led us to set up camp near here; on the other side of the hill. Since we were so close to Wiltshire, I decided we must visit our friends who we have not seen in months."

"How kind of you to interrupt your hunt and come visit us. We have been graced with your presence and would like to invite you inside for food and drink so that you may rest before your long journey home," the Queen offered.

"Thank you for your generous offer. I accept!" King Henry informed the Queen. He couldn't turn down any offer of food. "My soldiers will remain here. Would you have someone see to my men and their horses."

"Of course. Cedric, would you please see that these men have enough to fill their bellies and the horses are attended to?"

"Yes, your majesty." And Cedric left in the direction of the kitchen.

"Please follow me, King Henry. I look forward to hearing news of your kingdom and especially your wife and children." Queen Marianne beckoned to King Henry to follow her into the palace.

The Queen, John, and Arius led the King into the Great Hall where the servants had already set the table with an abundance of inviting food choices. The mix of aromas wafted through the room. They sat down with the Queen at the head of the table, King Henry on her left and John and Arius on her right. Queen Marianne knew she needed to be patient and hoped that the King would disclose the real reason for the visit during the course of the conversation.

There was a lot of small talk at first. The usual inquiries about health and family. And then, King Henry began to ask leading questions.

"You told me outside you would explain where the rest of your family is. It surprises me that King William is not among us."

"Aye, I am truly sorry for the delay in the explanation. King William has taken ill and is resting in his bed and has not been able to get up for many days now."

"It distresses me to hear that. May I be of some assistance for you and your family, maybe send over my personal physician?"

"Thank you for your offer, but the physician to the King is at his side and also Arius helps when he can. Is that not right, Arius?"

"Oh, aye! I have been able to help the King sleep better so his body can have more strength to fight the illness."

"That is good, that is very good.... Now that you have mentioned Arius, one of my soldiers informed me when he returned from his usual sweep of the countryside, that he thought he saw Arius appear behind a young rider whose horse was clearly out of control, was able to stop the horse and then they all just vanished. He was not however, able to identity the young man. I told my soldier it could not have been Prince John or Prince James since both are excellent horseman. So, I was wondering if you could enlighten me as to what my soldier shared with me."

"Yes, I would since Arius disclosed it to me as soon as he had returned," the Queen declared. Then she relayed the fabricated story about the stable boy, hoping that would satisfy the King's curiosity.

"Ah, aye, a stable boy. No wonder the young boy was not recognized by my soldier. But it did seem strange that Arius would go to all that trouble for a stable boy."

"Well, your majesty, I can see things that no one else can and when I realized the stable boy had crossed over the hill into your kingdom at a full gallop, I decided it might look suspicious and thought it was important to help him return home." Arius added.

"Aye, I see. We would not want an incident to take place because of a stable boy, now would we?" He sat back in his chair, gave a satisfied burp and then continued his thought. "However, if he truly was a stable boy, and my soldiers had caught him, then he would have been returned since it was surely an accident that the horse was uncontrollable." King Henry was not convinced that the story about the stable boy was true. But try as he could, Queen Marianne and Arius stuck to the story without any deviations.

"In the absence of my father, since he is upstairs ill at the moment, I must ask you if there is anything we can do for you before you take your leave of us," Prince John inquired as he hoped they would take the hint and leave.

"I am sorry I did not get to see King William on this visit, but maybe I can return soon to check his progress, as I am concerned about his illness."

"Of course, we would welcome another visit from a concerned friend and look forward to the continued goodwill between our kingdoms." On the outside, the Queen appeared calm in her demeanor, but on the inside, she was screaming, 'Please go home and stop this interrogation.'

Meanwhile, the soldiers in the courtyard, were constantly scanning the perimeter of the castle for signs of anything different or for anyone who didn't seem to belong. Nothing caught their eye. But one soldier decided to accompany the horses to the stable to make sure they were attended to properly. He was the soldier who had witnessed the incident with Luke and Arius. While there, he started talking to one of the stable boys and casually mentioned what he had seen and stated he was concerned as to the boy's welfare. The stable boy said he didn't have any firsthand knowledge of the event, but had heard that one of the other stable boys had gotten into trouble while exercising a horse and is fine thanks to Arius. The soldier thanked him for taking care of the horses and asked that the horses be returned as soon as they had been watered. The soldier then returned to the courtyard satisfied that he had been told the truth about the incident he had seen.

"Thank you for your generous gift of food and drink. It was good to be able to fill my belly after our long journey. Now I must be on my way back to my kingdom. It is not good to stay away too long."

"I will tell Father that you graced us with your presence while on one of your hunting trips and that you inquired after him. I know he will find your concern comforting." Prince John mentioned as they walked the King out.

"Aye, please do. We must not wait so long between visits next time." King Henry proceeded to go out into the courtyard and attempted to mount his horse. Arius had to turn his head and act like he was coughing because he found himself laughing at the King's feeble attempt to get on his horse. Because King Henry couldn't get his leg up high enough to put his foot in the stirrup, he had to ask one of his soldiers for assistance and was finally able to swing his leg over the saddle. Once the King was on his horse, the soldiers climbed onto their horses and waited for instructions from the King. "Please send word when William has recovered so that I may return for another visit. Wish him well from me, please."

"Safe travels to you and your men." Queen Marianne nodded.

"Our visit is completed and now we must return home," King Henry announced to the soldiers. And he turned his horse toward the castle gate. Then he leaned toward the captain of the guard, "I think there is something amiss here, but I can't put my finger on it. I need you to assign two soldiers to remain here, stay out of sight, and maintain a watchful eye for anything out of the ordinary."

"Aye, sir. Will do."

As they were leaving the castle, two of the soldiers broke off and disappeared into a dark corner. The rest of the group rode out through the gate and left Wiltshire.

Once they were out of sight, Queen Marianne immediately turned around and let out a large sigh. "I am so glad he has departed. I hope we were able to convince him that it was a stable boy that his soldier saw and not Luke. And it is a good thing the King did not notice you found his mounting skills laughable, Arius!" And she covered her mouth for she had to laugh, too.

"Sorry, your majesty, but it could not be helped!"

"I thought you did very well, Mother. You appeared calm when you spoke to him, not at all nervous," John affirmed.

"I was very nervous indeed and had to hold my hands together for fear I would start shaking. I hope your father comes home to us soon. We are doing our best to hold this kingdom together, but I worry if he is gone too long there may be problems within and without the kingdom."

"Oh, Mother! We have forgotten about those that are in hiding! Please excuse me and I will go and tell them it is safe to come out."

"Thank you, John. We do need to let them know that it is safe now and let them know of the visit."

And John left.

"Do you need me anymore, your majesty?" Arius asked.

"No, Arius, you may leave. But know, while my husband is gone, that I may call upon you at any time if needed. I also want you to stay by Luke anytime he is out and about within the castle walls."

"Aye, your majesty." Then Arius departed leaving the Queen by herself. She walked into the palace, found a chair, plopped down in it and then started to cry, quietly.

# CHAPTER 28

## THE PLAN TO RETURN

"I found Dr. Ross and told him you are inquiring as to how long it will be before we can return home," Prince James announced to his father as he entered the hospital room. "He said he would come as soon as he could."

King William was sitting up in bed glancing at a magazine that had been left in the room. When he turned toward James, he had a look of alarm on his face.

"What is this? It is very peculiar. How do they get all of these people and things on this paper? This must be black magic!" he declared as he threw the magazine on the floor.

"That is called a magazine. The people of this time put pictures on paper and they like to look at them." Gretchen threw in.

"Father, it will not hurt you. I asked the same question of Justine. She tried to explain it to me but I found it rather confusing." Then James reached down and picked up the magazine. "See, it will not hurt you and these are not real people."

"I have decided not to have anything to do with it, so please put it on the other side of the room," the King announced. "Thank you, James for relaying my question to Dr. Ross. We must depart here soon!" King

William was very anxious to return to his kingdom. He didn't like knowing that the Queen and Prince John had been left to make decisions in his absence. It wasn't that he didn't trust them, he felt guilty for having placed so much responsibility on them, plus the fact that he wasn't around to advise them if they needed it.

Dr. Ross pushed the room door open and walked over to the side of the bed. He grabbed the chair near him, pulled it close to the bad and sat down.

"So how is our patient today?"

"In excellent health, thank you."

"King William, James has informed me that you would like to be discharged and return home ASAP..., sorry, as soon as possible. It's important, if I allow this, that we be able to transport any medicine or equipment I might need for at home care. I certainly don't want you to relapse. You have been progressing very nicely up to this point, which is very important. But you must understand that the trip back will certainly be harder than it was getting here."

"Please do whatever you can so that I may return to Wiltshire very soon."

"Let me evaluate your current condition and we will see. Once I give you the all clear to be discharged, we will need to leave. So, you must give me some time to gather medicine and portable equipment for the trip back."

"I agree with this reasoning, and I thank you. James, will help you with anything you may need? And, Gretchen also offers her services if needed."

"Certainly, Father," James nodded. "Justine and I would be most honored to help Dr. Ross. By the way, where is Justine, sir?"

"She is making sure we have clean clothes for the journey back. We certainly can't return in scrubs! Now let me get started on this exam." Dr. Ross began his examination and made notes of anything he might need once they returned to Wiltshire.

'Okay, that should do it! I've done some calculations and I think it would be wise to remain in the hospital one more day so that you can gain some more strength and I will have time to pack up any supplies and figure out how we are going to get back to Stonehenge."

"One more day will be acceptable," King William acknowledged.

"Gretchen, please continue to keep an eye on the King and alert Justine if you need anything." He knew she was there even if he couldn't see her.

"King William, please advise Dr. Ross that we will need to travel at night so as not to be seen when we open the portal," Gretchen declared.

"Dr. Ross, Gretchen has informed me that we will need to travel at night so there are no witnesses when the portal is opened."

"Then, we will leave tomorrow night. I will discharge you around 5:00 pm. I will have everything packed and ready for the trip back. The trip to Stonehenge will be about an hour. I should probably rent a van to make sure we are able to transport all of us and any needed medical equipment."

"Do what?" asked the King.

"Oh, I'm sorry, I was talking out loud. Please don't worry about a thing. I will arrange everything. Just be prepared to leave tomorrow night. James, I need you to come with me, please."

"Aye, sir. Father, I will return later. And Gretchen, take good care of him."

James and Dr. Ross left the room to make preparations for the journey back to Wiltshire. Dr. Ross wrote a prescription for the King for medicine he would need for the next couple of weeks and a little extra. He also ordered antibiotics since he remembered that Dr. Lange had used up his supply. "James, will you please take these prescriptions to the hospital pharmacy and have them filled?"

"But I have no knowledge of how to do that!" he exclaimed.

"I'm sorry, I keep forgetting you don't live in this century!" Dr. Ross admitted. "All right, you will need to find Justine and have her accompany you. She will know what to do." So, Dr. Ross told James how to locate Justine and sent him on his way. One thing was now checked off his list. Next, he asked someone in the hospital where he might be able to rent a van and found one about two blocks from the hospital.

Now, he had to figure out a way to take an electrocardiogram. But he couldn't take one of the newer models because those ran off a computer. He decided to ask someone if there might be somewhere in the hospital where obsolete equipment was stored. If he could find an old one, that would be great. But that may be something he would have to do without. He knew there was electricity in Wiltshire, so he should be able to hook it up and use it. He inquired and found out there was a room in the basement for such items. He told them he needed it for some research he was doing and asked that he might be able to borrow it. He was told he could have whatever he wanted since it would eventually be tossed out anyway. He went to the supply room in the basement of the hospital and felt like he was on a scavenger hunt! Everything smelled old and musty as he searched the shelves. Not only did he find what he was looking for, but was able to locate several other portable items that could be used for other purposes. He was glad he didn't have to requisition any of it because he didn't want to return it.

# CHAPTER 29

## THE SYMPOSIUM!

Dr. Ross worked through the night and was now almost ready for the return trip. As he was making preparations for the journey, it suddenly dawned on him that dates and time had been a blur since that day at Stonehenge and he had no idea what day of the week it was. They had been in Oxford for a week now and he hadn't even bothered to check the date or his phone for that matter. He had turned it off when they were in Wiltshire because there wasn't any service there. He decided to turn his phone back on and it started pinging like crazy. There were several messages from the group that had organized the symposium and he had missed all of them! Oh no! He had totally forgotten about the symposium! He checked the date on his phone and realized that the symposium was that very day and they were returning to Wiltshire that evening! What was he to do now? It was still early so maybe he could get to London, do the symposium and then get back to Oxford in time to take the group to Stonehenge. But he hadn't even prepared for this. What was he going to say? As he thought about it, it occurred to him that he could use the King's illness as one of his examples since that was fresh in his mind, but update the time period of course. He had been gathering supplies all night, hadn't slept and was very tired. But this was something he had to do. He was their main presenter! And, it was the reason for the trip to London in the first place! He went to find Justine, who was sleeping in their assigned room.

"Justine, wake up!"

"What, huh, oh my gosh, Dad, what time is it?"

"It's 5:30."

"5:30? AM?" And Justine turned over and put the pillow over her head. Then she mumbled, "I hope you have a good reason for waking me up out of a perfectly wonderful dream!"

"I do. Please listen." Justine removed the pillow and turned back over to face her dad. "With all that has happened in the past week or so, I had all but forgotten about the symposium until about an hour ago."

"The symposium? Oh, good grief, Dad! Why are you even considering going to that? We're going back to Wiltshire tonight!"

"I know, but I think I can do both. London is only fifty-eight miles away so if I leave soon, I'll be able to make it in plenty of time. You need to hold down the fort while I'm gone and call me immediately if anything happens.".

"Okay, I will. But Dad, have you even slept, and more importantly, do you know what you're going to say?"

"I decided that I would use the King's case as an example during my speech and I can prepare anything else on the way to London."

"Oh, wow! I can't believe this!"

"You'll be fine. Just don't panic."

"That's easy for you to say."

"Where are the clothes you washed? I will need to wear them. I hope I'll have time to stop at the hotel so I can put on a suit. Oh, wow! The hotel...! I bet they've been wondering about us, too! I'll need to come up with a good story regarding our whereabouts for the past week."

"Yes, you will. Good luck with that!" Justine shrugged. Then her eyes got really big and she yelled, "Oh no! Dad, I just remembered, you can only be a mile away from Gretchen at any time or you'll forget everything! You won't know where you've been or where we are. You can't go! There's no way you're leaving here!"

"I forgot all about that. It's a good thing you remembered! I was going to leave without waking you. Boy, that would have been a huge mistake! Now what do I do?"

"Is there any way you can do a live feed from here?"

"I don't know? That might work. I'm sure the hospital has a conference room somewhere. We need to check with Gretchen to make sure I can't leave; then we need to check with the hospital. I should probably call the hotel and let them know we're in Oxford."

"I know," Justine asserted. "We could use the fact that you had to operate on the King as your reason for not being in London! We could say that we were sightseeing and someone collapsed and you had to do surgery on him. And all of that is true!"

"Good thinking, young lady! Now, let's go find Gretchen so we can verify whether or not I can leave and we'll go from there."

"Wait, Dad! You forgot that I can communicate with Gretchen. I can ask her to meet us somewhere since we don't want to wake the King."

"Okay, do that!"

Justine got up and threw on some clothes. She didn't have to look for the necklace because she never took it off.

"Gretchen, can you hear me?" She waited for a minute, no answer. "Gretchen, wake up! I need you!"

"No need to yell. I can hear you. What can I do for you at this early hour?"

"My dad and I need to talk to you. Can you meet us in the waiting room near the King's room, please?"

"Yes, I will be there."

"Okay, we'll be there in about two minutes."

So, Justine and her dad got on the elevator and got off on the tenth floor. As they walked past the nurse's station, they nodded, and walked on to the waiting room.

"I am here, Miss Justine. What is so important that it could not wait?"

"Go ahead, Dad. Tell Gretchen your plan and I'll be the go-between."

Dr. Ross told her what had happened and that he was planning to travel to London that day to speak at the symposium and then return in time for them to go to Stonehenge. He wanted to know if that would be possible.

"No, Dr. Ross. It is not possible for you to leave. You will lose all memory of us and of Wiltshire. You will not remember to return."

"Would I be able to go with him?" Justine asked. "I have the necklace and I would still remember, right?"

"I think London may be too far for the necklace to work and I do not want to take any chances. I would not be able to accompany you because I must stay with the royal family. You must stay here. There is no other way."

"I told you, Dad. You can't go. You'll have to look into the other option we talked about."

"All right. I'll contact the organizers and tell them what happened. They may be happy that I've been able to put my skills to good use here in England." Dr. Ross admitted. "I need to talk to a hospital administrator, tell them my predicament, and see if they can help me find a solution."

1 3 8

"Well, it is 6:00 am now, so maybe someone is awake?" Justine pointed out.

"I hope so, but if not, I guess they will be soon! Thank you, Gretchen. I'll see you later."

Dr. Ross walked over to the nurse's station and inquired about contacting an administrator so he could resolve this situation. The nurse needed to know the reason for the request before she could give him the phone number. He explained about the symposium and that he was to give a speech that afternoon. She decided it wouldn't be against hospital policy, so she wrote the phone number on a piece of paper for him. Then she wished him good luck.

Dr. Ross located a phone he could use and called Dr. Robinson, the hospital administrator. Dr. Robinson didn't answer the phone right away so Dr. Ross assumed he was probably still asleep. He figured correctly! When Dr. Robinson finally answered, he introduced himself and told Dr. Robinson about the circumstances that led to his being in Oxford when he was supposed to be in London. Dr. Robinson listened without giving any indication as to how he might reply. When Dr. Ross was finished, there was a pause on the other end of the line leaving Dr. Ross wondering what was to come next.

"You say your name is Dr. Andrew Ross, noted heart surgeon from the United States, and you are supposed to speak at a symposium in London today. Is that correct?"

"Correct."

"And that you currently have a patient in my hospital and can't leave."

"Correct again."

"Well, that's not a good situation to be in is it?"

"No, sir, it's not."

"I guess we're just going to have to do something about that! Especially since I was supposed to be traveling to London today to hear you speak!"

"You are, I mean were?"

"Yes, I was. But what could be better than to be the only one able to hear your speech in person!"

"That is fantastic, Dr. Robinson! Then I'm assuming you have a conference room that we can utilize so I can deliver my speech here?"

"We do. I will meet you in about an hour and we can get that ready."

"Thank you! You don't know how much I appreciate this. Now I need to contact the organizers and let them know what's happened and that we will live stream the speech from here."

"Sounds like a plan. See you in an hour." Dr. Robinson hung up the phone and Dr. Ross breathed a sigh of relief. Now all he had to do was figure out what he was going to say. But first, he needed to alert London and, if possible, call their hotel.

An hour later, Dr. Robinson met Dr. Ross in the conference room where the speech would be delivered. Dr. Ross had changed into the clean clothes Justine had washed and was ready to go. They set up the computer and the video camera and ran a test to make sure the feed was going through to the room where the symposium was to take place and that the sound was working. Once that was done, Dr. Ross thanked Dr. Robinson for his help and excused himself because he still needed to work on his presentation. He found a quiet area near the conference room so he could put his thoughts together.

"Hey, Dad! How's it going?" Justine stated as she peeked around the door. "I came to hear your speech! I can't believe I can finally see what you're all about!" Justine said excitedly. "I brought James along so he could witness another modern miracle!"

"Dr. Ross, I hope it will not be a problem for you if we watch you speak." James stated.

"No, no. I'm glad you two are here along with Dr. Robinson. Now I won't feel so alone talking to people who are 60 miles away!"

"Even though Justine has told me all that I am to see, I am still not sure how this works or what I will see. But I am looking forward to it."

"Me, too!" Dr. Ross added. "It is 12:30 right now and the symposium starts at 1:00. We'd better move to the conference room so I'm ready to go!"

When they got to the conference room, Dr. Ross introduced Justine and James to Dr. Robinson.

"It's very nice to meet you. I'm very honored to have your father working here in this hospital right now, Justine. I wish I had known sooner that he was here. I have been following his career for many years now. I would love to have him on staff here but I know he is committed to working at the hospital in Indianapolis."

"Thank you, Dr. Robinson, for your compliments. I am humbled to be here, in your hospital, for I know of your commitment to this hospital and to your patients, and am sorry I didn't realize I was operating in your hospital until now."

"Well, I feel privileged to finally get to meet you in person. Now, I won't bother you anymore since you need to give a speech!"

Then the three of them, Dr. Robinson, Justine, and James sat down at the table across from Dr. Ross to wait for the symposium to begin. Dr. Ross logged in as he was told to do and was able to see the audience arriving since the camera was not on him at the moment. As soon as everyone was seated, he heard someone introduce him and then proceed to acknowledge his many accomplishments over the years: where he had worked and currently works, articles he had written, books he had published, and awards he had received from the American Medical Association for his work in heart research. At that moment, Justine wanted to get up and cheer! She didn't know "her dad" had accomplished so much. To her, he was just Dad, but he was something a whole lot different to the medical community.

Dr. Ross stood patiently during the introduction. When the speaker was done, the audience erupted into applause and stood up. Dr. Ross was a humble person and his face grew red as he waited for the applause to subside. He put his hands up as a signal to please sit down and then thanked them for the praise they had heaped on him. But he wanted them to know that there were many who were instrumental in his success and he wanted to acknowledge that without them, none of this would have been possible. Then he apologized for not being with them in person and explained the circumstances that led to his being in Oxford. Which of course, was not the complete truth! Then he delivered his speech.

Justine and James remained very quiet throughout the speech. Justine sat there marveling at the knowledge her dad was imparting to this room full of prestigious individuals in the medical field. She had a grin on her face that stretched from ear to ear during the whole speech. She was beaming with pride. James, on the other hand, sat wide-eyed throughout the speech trying to take in everything that was happening. There were several times he wanted to stop everything and ask questions but knew he had to keep silent.

Finally, Dr. Ross was done and he signed off. Dr. Robinson immediately got up and shook his hand, praising him for delivering such an interesting speech. He informed Dr. Ross that his staff at the hospital would greatly benefit from the knowledge that was shared.

When Dr. Robinson had finished, Justine got up and gave her dad a big hug. "I'm so proud of you, Dad," she whispered.

"Thank you. I'm just doing what I think is important in helping to save lives."

"Dr. Ross! What I have seen here today is beyond my understanding but I found you to be an inspiration. I am glad beyond words that Gretchen brought you to us. You are of great importance to so many people!" James declared as he stood there in awe.

"I want to thank you both for being here. It meant a lot to me. Now, we need to think about getting your dad home.

"Oh, you're leaving us?" Dr. Robinson asked.

"Yes, we are. I need to accompany my patient tonight as he returns home. He lives somewhere difficult to reach and therefore he may not receive the medical care needed as he recovers from his surgery."

"Well, that is certainly going above and beyond your duties as a physician. But that's what makes you who you are. We are very honored you chose to bring your patient to our hospital and welcome you back any time. Have you ever thought about teaching? I would be honored to have you return to Oxford sometime to impart all of your knowledge to our students! Just think about it. You don't have to give me an answer right now."

"Thank you for the offer, Dr. Robinson. I will give it some thought." Then Dr. Robinson shook Dr. Ross's hand and left.

"Okay, you two. Let's get busy. We have a King to deliver home!"

"Does that mean you might return someday, Justine?" Prince James hoped.

"I have no idea. But I think I would like it if we did."

# CHAPTER 30

## SPIES IN THE CASTLE!

"My lady! I must speak with you!" Queen Marianne looked up and saw the Captain of the Guard standing in front of her. She pulled herself together and stood up.

"Yes, what is it?"

"Your majesty, I think we have a problem."

"Well, please tell me. What has happened?"

"King Henry entered the castle with ten soldiers, but he left with only eight. Two of them must still be within the castle walls somewhere. I fear he left them as spies, your Majesty."

"Oh, that will not do! That will not do at all! We must find them! I am so thankful that the villagers know they are to keep things hidden until the bell rings to let them know everything is clear." The Queen was distraught and needed closure as soon as possible. "Alert every soldier we have and tell them to search every space, large or small, until they are found. These spies must not discover our secrets or see the visitors. It would mean disaster for our way of life and could possibly destroy the peace in our country."

"We will find them, your majesty. I promise!" Then the Captain quickly departed the palace to dispatch his men to every corner of the castle.

"John, where are you?" the Queen yelled as she moved about the palace. "I need you right now!"

"Right here, Mother." John replied as he came down the hallway. He was followed by Luke, Mrs. Ross, Madison, and Bethany. "You sent me to fetch them. I told them everything was fine and they could come out of hiding.

"Well, everything is not fine. And we must have a plan right away. Please follow me to the throne room where we can discuss this in private."

"Aye, Mother." As the Queen walked away, John turned his attention to Madison and Bethany. "I need you two to go to your rooms and stay there until I come get you."

"What happened, John? You just came to tell us we could come out." Madison inquired.

"I know I did. But something happened that has upset our mother. I am not aware yet what that may be. Therefore, please stay put until I find out. And Mrs. Ross, you and Luke will need to remain in your rooms as well. I will inform you of the problem as soon as I can."

John then left the four of them standing in the hallway as he went to meet his mother in the throne room.

"We should not have taken that horseback ride!" Bethany whined. "Then none of this would have happened," she said as she started to cry.

"It wasn't your fault," Luke assured her. "I should never have decided to try to race you all to the top of the hill. I don't know what I was thinking. That's just it! I guess I wasn't thinking."

"None of that matters now," Mrs. Ross pointed out. "You can't cry over spilled milk."

"What? We did not spill any milk," Madison quickly replied.

"Oh, no. I don't mean you actually... what I meant to say was that what is past is past and you can't change

145

that now. We need to deal with what is now. So, let's go to our rooms and wait for John to tell us what to do next."

"All right, but may we stay with you and Luke for right now," Bethany begged. "I am scared and there is nothing to do in our room."

"Why don't we all go stay in your room and keep each other company?" Luke suggested.

"That would be wonderful, thank you." Madison added.

So, the four of them retreated to Bethany's room to wait for John.

John entered the throne room and walked over to his mother. She was seated in her chair next to her husband's throne.

"I wish he were here. He would know what to do," the Queen noted as she placed her hand on the King's throne.

"What happened, Mother? You must tell me!" John blurted out.

When she looked at him, it was as if she were somewhere else. She was looking in his direction but it was like he wasn't there.

"Mother! What is wrong?"

That startled her out of her inner thoughts and she straightened up and looked right at him. She explained that after King Henry left the castle, the Captain of the Guard sought her out to inform her that when King Henry arrived, he had ten soldiers with him but left with only eight. Currently, these two soldiers were somewhere within the castle walls. She told him she had ordered the Captain to gather all soldiers and search every inch of the castle grounds until they were found. She also told him that since the "all clear" bell had not been rung yet the villagers should still have everything hidden. She was hoping the unwanted soldiers would be found soon.

"I must do my part and help find these men." John exclaimed. "We must have every able-bodied person to help with this search, even villagers."

"Aye, we must! I will go tell our guests, and the girls, to remain in the castle no matter what they see or hear. You need to find the Captain and have him ask trusted villagers to aide in the search."

"Aye, Mother. I will go right away." John left the throne room with three goals: to locate the Captain, to see how the search was progressing, and to assign some villagers to help.

Once outside the palace, he noticed that life seemed to be calm around the castle. The villagers were going about their business as usual as if nothing had happened. He asked one of the men near him if he had seen the Captain. He had and told Prince John where to find him. As he was moving in that direction, a child on a bicycle rode by right in front of him and he ran after the child, grabbed the bike, and told him to put it away immediately. He looked around to see if anyone might be watching and didn't see a strange face. But that didn't mean anything. King Henry's spies could be hiding anywhere. The child disappeared into a nearby house and John continued on.

"Did you see what I saw?" One of the spies had just seen the child on the bicycle and posed the question to the other soldier.

"No, what might that be?"

"There was a child riding something that was very strange. I have never seen one before."

"Well, out with it then, what did it look like?"

"It had two wheels and a seat and a child was riding on it."

"I think your mind is playing tricks on you. I did not see it and I was standing right beside you."

"Well, King Henry asked us to watch for anything. Maybe I was just hoping to see something and it was my imagination. But then again, I could not imagine what I just saw."

"Let us keep looking so we can leave here and report back to the King." The two soldiers then disappeared into the shadow of a nearby house.

After seeing the bicycle, Prince John became worried that other items would begin appearing. He looked up to make sure the electrical wires were still hidden. He didn't see any which was a good sign. He continued to follow the dirt path between the houses, went around a corner and found the Captain.

"Prince John, may I ask what you are doing outside the palace?"

"Yes, Captain. I am here at the request of my mother, the Queen. I am to assist you in your search. We are also asking that you seek the help of trusted villagers so that these spies may be located swiftly."

"There are many soldiers searching at this very moment. I ordered several to remain on the castle walls giving them a better vantage point from up there. Also, I did not want to leave the castle walls unguarded."

"Captain, I came across a child riding a bicycle on my way to find you. It is my hope it was not seen by one of the spies, but I cannot be sure."

"We will find them, Prince John. They will not get beyond the castle walls." The Captain said with confidence.

"What can I do to help? Where have you not looked? I can start there."

"I will go with you, my Prince. You should not go by yourself. We have not searched the stables yet."

"Then we will go to the stables. On the way there we can alert some of the villagers and ask them to be vigilant."

The Captain and Prince John proceeded to go to the stable area. There were some villagers out and about on the way there, so they stopped and asked them if they had seen any soldiers dressed in different armor lurking about. They said they had not but would keep an eye out for them. As they got closer to the stables, they heard horses whinnying and what sounded like a scuffle. They immediately crouched down and hid behind some bushes. They both pulled their swords from their sheaths and proceeded very cautiously. When they got to the barn door, they stood up one on either side of the door. The Captain peered ever so carefully around the edge of the door to get a quick 180 of the insides of the barn. He observed several figures at the other end of the barn who seemed to be fighting. But it was hard to discern who they were. Since the door was unguarded, the Captain signaled to Prince John to enter but to keep low and stay quiet. They both moved to opposite sides inside the door at the same time and stood up against the walls. Both were in the shadows and the figures on the other end didn't seem to notice.

"You are not getting out of here," came a cry at the other end of the barn.

Then they heard the sound of metal clashing against metal and realized that two of the figures were the soldiers they were seeking. They both rushed forward and joined the fight. When they arrived at the other end of the barn, they realized the soldiers were fighting two of the stable boys. Now there were four fighting against the two. Even though one of the stable boys had been injured on his left arm, he still found the strength to keep fighting. Prince John motioned to the injured boy to back away. The soldiers were not going to give up and continued to thrust their swords at anyone near them. Prince John had become an excellent swordsman and was holding his own. The Captain was able to injure one of the soldiers on his right leg causing him to fall to the ground. But as he fell, he thrust his sword at the Captain and injured him in the stomach. Prince John jumped in to stop the soldier from injuring the Captain further. He grabbed the arm of the Captain and held him up with his left arm while he continued to fight with his right arm. Meanwhile, the other stable boy had crawled off to the side away from the sword because he, too, had been injured. Now, it was just Prince John. The remaining soldier grabbed his companion who was on the ground, moved the two of them toward the door in the back of the stable, opened it and left. Prince John wasn't able to pursue them since he now had a very heavy Captain hanging on his left arm and there were also two injured stable boys. He was able to get the Captain to a bale of hay that was nearby and laid him down very carefully.

"Don't move, Captain. And you two boys stay where you are as well. I will go get our physician."

Prince John ran out the front door toward the palace. On the way, he ordered two soldiers he came across to go to the stable and remain there until he returned. He ran as fast as he could and finally got to the palace. Once inside, he ran to Dr. Lange's office. He alerted Dr. Lange to the situation and asked Dr. Lange to go with him to the stables. Dr. Lange gathered supplies, put them in his doctor's bag and left with Prince John. On the way out of the palace, Dr. Lange grabbed a bottle of whiskey in case it was needed. The Queen saw them as they were leaving and asked what had happened.

"I cannot talk to you now, Mother. I will explain everything when I get back. Right now, it is important that I get Dr. Lange to the stables as soon as possible. The Captain is injured."

Prince John didn't wait for a response from the Queen. He darted out the door and the two of them ran as fast as they could to the stable. Once they arrived, Dr. Lange assessed the situation and attended to the Captain first. While trying to stop the bleeding, he also ordered the two soldiers to get some supplies out of his bag and wrap the leg of the injured stable boy. The other boy's wound was superficial and could wait.

"I'm going to need to close this cut or the Captain will continue to bleed. I need your help, Prince John."

They moved the Captain to a table in a somewhat clean area of the stable. They were in luck since the Captain had passed out while they were moving him. Dr. Lange checked the wound to see what damage had been done and was glad to see that the sword had missed the major organs. Once he had done that, he started working as fast as he could to repair the damage. He used the whiskey to help clean the cut as he worked. He was finally able to close all affected areas and then closed the cut itself. Then he poured more whiskey on top of the wound to guard against infection. Once he had finished with the Captain, he checked the stable boys and stitched up their wounds as well.

"We need to get the Captain to the palace where I can continue to look after him. We will need a stretcher."

"One of you soldiers, go get a stretcher for Dr. Lange," Prince John ordered. "Then you will need to help carry the Captain to the palace. You will also need to locate two more soldiers to help these stable boys back to their homes."

"Aye, Prince John. I know where we can find a stretcher. We should return soon." And the two soldiers left. They returned with the stretcher and two more soldiers. The Captain, who was still unconscious, was placed on the stretcher and carried very carefully to the palace. They took him to Dr. Lange's office and laid him on the bed. Then they left to make sure the stable boys had safely gotten to their homes.

"I need to tell my mother what has happened. You stay here and take good care of the Captain. Please, nothing can happen to him."

"He is still unconscious and I need to monitor him until I know he is fine. I have some medicine that I need to give him to make sure he doesn't get an infection. I'll let you know his condition when he wakes up."

"Thank you, Dr. Lange. We are blessed that you decided to remain in Wiltshire." Then Prince John gave Dr. Lange a nod and left to go find his mother.

# CHAPTER 31

## THE TRIP HOME

Now that the symposium was over, Dr. Ross was ready to turn his attention to returning James and the King home to Wiltshire. First, he needed the van he had rented so they could load it. It was supposed to be delivered within the next half hour or so. It was being delivered because it was more than a mile away from the hospital which meant he couldn't pick it up himself. Also, he requested that someone come pick it up at Stonehenge because he wasn't sure when he and his family would be returning to modern day England. That would depend on his patient. He had everything waiting at the loading ramp in the back of the hospital. James and Justine had just left the King and were there to help. The van finally arrived and they started loading everything. Dr. Ross had personally chosen several items from the obsolete medical equipment stored in the basement of the hospital. He was told he could take anything he wanted, so he did. Now he was afraid he might not be able to get all of it and the passengers in the van.

It took all three of them about a half hour, but they were able to get it all in and still leave enough seats for the passengers. Next on his list was to discharge the King so the King could leave the hospital. He locked the van, and the three of them went up the elevator to the tenth floor for the last time. They went to the King's room and found him already dressed and waiting.

"Well, your time in 2020 England is almost all over, King William. I'm so glad we were able to get you to a hospital. I don't think I could have successfully completed that surgery without the help of everything that was available to me here."

"Thank you, Dr. Ross for everything. Now we need to get me back to my family and kingdom as soon as you can."

"I'll just fill out the discharge paperwork and we will be ready. Oh, by the way, so you won't be surprised, a nurse will be coming to get you with a chair on wheels. It's called a wheelchair and she is in charge of making sure you arrive safely to the van. It's hospital rules. The van, your carriage, is loaded and waiting for you in back of the hospital. Please don't give her any trouble. And try to hold off asking any questions until you're in the van."

"A wheelchair? I am anxious to see this special chair."

"Gretchen, please make sure he behaves. We only have from here to the loading dock to go and then we're home free."

"Gretchen says she will monitor the King's behavior," Justine offered.

"Okay, thanks. Now, make sure you have picked up everything that is ours. I will go sign the papers and the nurse should be here soon. Everyone, please come down together. I'll meet you at the van."

"James," Justine began, "Your father was asleep the whole trip here and has since only seen his hospital room and the hall. It will be interesting to see how he reacts to all the things around him once we leave."

"That is true! That thought did not cross my mind until now!" James blurted out. "I wonder if he will react in the same way I did on the way here! You are right, this will be very interesting."

"Gretchen said she can't wait either," Justine added.

The door opened and a nurse came in with the wheelchair. She positioned it by the side of the bed so it would be easy for King William to maneuver.

"So, this is the chair with wheels. Very interesting. What do you call it? Oh, aye, a wheelchair. Fitting name for this invention!" King William was amused by this new item.

"Aye, Father, it is a wheelchair. You need to get into it so we can leave."

The nurse tried to assist him as he was moving from the bed into the wheelchair, but King William declared that he could do it himself. So, the nurse backed up and just held the chair in place. Then the nurse put the foot rests down and asked him to placed his feet on them. While the nurse was pushing the King out into the hallway, he declared that he must have one of these and wanted to know where he could get one. The nurse told him he might be able to get one at a medical supply store. James and Justine started laughing very quietly to each other as they witnessed the first of many surprises.

"Gretchen, please describe an elevator to Mr. Pendragon," Justine said as they proceeded down the hallway to the elevators. She wanted to prepare him for what was coming next.

"Gretchen? That's not my name. It's Lydia." The nurse shared as she pushed the King.

"Oh, I'm sorry I got your name wrong. Thank you, Lydia, for your help." Justine apologized. Then she heard Gretchen trying to explain to the King about an elevator and she could see that the King had no idea what she was talking about.

The nurse wheeled him to the elevator and pushed the down button. When the doors opened, the King just about jumped out of the chair!

"What is that! Is this more magic?"

"Sorry, Lydia. Hard as it is to believe, but he's never been on an elevator before. This is all new to him!" Justine had never spoken more truer words in her life!

"Never? I find that hard to believe. Doesn't he ever go anywhere?" Lydia inquired.

"Yes, but it is somewhere that has stairs." James admitted.

"And on the farm, where he doesn't need any elevators," Justine pointed out.

The door closed and the elevator began to go down. The King had the same reaction that James had had when he first encountered the elevator. He started laughing and looking out the window at the scenery.

"I would like to ride on this again, if I may," the King roared.

"Sorry, Father, this is a one-time trip for you."

The doors opened, they all got off and moved toward the loading dock. Dr. Ross was waiting for them there.

"Dr. Ross, I think your patient needs to get out more. His son told me that he's never been on an elevator."

"Dad, remember? He hasn't been too far from the farm his whole life and hasn't experienced city life."

"Ah, yes, that's true. Sad to say. He's had so much to do on the farm. No time for vacations either." Dr. Ross followed Justine's lead.

"Well, here is your patient, doctor. I hope he enjoyed his first trip to the city." Nurse Lydia quipped.

"Thank you, nurse. I'll take it from here." And Dr. Ross helped the King into the front seat of the van. As he was doing that, he whispered to him as a reminder to please not say anything until the nurse was gone.

The nurse took the wheelchair and walked back into the building. Once she was gone, James and Justine couldn't contain themselves any longer and burst into laughter.

"James, why are you laughing?" King William asked.

"Sorry, Father. I am laughing because you are reacting to things the same way I did when we left Stonehenge. Please know that I am not laughing at you, but at us. None of this is like anything in Wiltshire, even when Arius does his magic."

"Please forgive me if I ask too many questions." The King requested.

"Ask away, your majesty. There can never be too many questions from you and James," Dr. Ross replied.

Dr. Ross spoke too soon because the trip became one question after another. Dr. Ross, Justine, and Gretchen all tried to take turns answering the myriad questions from the visitors from the 16th century. But those questions sure helped to pass the time and the hour trip seemed to go very quickly. Before they knew it, Stonehenge was in sight and it was just starting to get dark.

Dr. Ross surveyed their surroundings and didn't see anyone or any cars in the area. He knew he was going to have to drive the van up as close as he could even though the area around Stonehenge was blocked off. He also knew that no visitors were allowed near it anymore. Gretchen pointed out a side path of gravel leading up to the place where they had been standing during the tour a week ago. Gretchen, via Justine, notified Dr. Ross that he could drive up the path and their tracks wouldn't be noticed. He did that and got as close as he could. Then they waited until the sky was completely dark to ensure no one would see them.

Once they felt it was safe. They began unloading the van and placing all of the equipment in front of the portal that would take them back to Wiltshire. The King remained in the van while they worked. When done, James and Dr. Ross helped the King out of the van and steadied him as they walked toward the stone. Justine and Gretchen, who was now visible, had already reached the stone and Gretchen had opened the portal. James and Dr. Ross continued through the portal to the other side where they sat the King down on a large stone.

As soon as the King was settled, James and Dr. Ross assisted Justine and Gretchen in transporting the equipment through the portal. Once everything had been moved, Gretchen closed the portal. Then she closed her eyes and, using her mind, contacted Arius so he could meet them there. She also informed him they would need a wagon to transport the items they brought with them back to the castle. It was still dark even on this side of the portal, which of course was to their benefit. The King was very tired and he lay down on the ground to rest while they waited for Arius to come. They heard the sound of hooves hitting the road and Arius, the wagon and a driver appeared.

"Welcome back to Wiltshire, your majesties." Arius said. Then he continued, "A lot has happened while you were away, King William, and I will apprise you of it all. But we will wait until you return to the castle."

"It is good to be back, Arius," the King admitted as he started to get up. "But I am concerned about this news you have to share with me. I am anxious to know what has transpired while I was gone. Please transport us to the castle at once."

"Yes, your majesty."

"Wait, we need to load this equipment on the wagon, first, Father," James announced. "Please wait until that is done."

"All right. Do it quickly."

It didn't take very long before the wagon was loaded and ready to go. As soon as the wagon started down the road, Arius said a chant and the five of them disappeared and reappeared in the Main Hall of the palace.

"Gretchen, will you keep watch for the wagon and make sure it returns safely?" the King asked.

"Yes, your majesty. I will let you know when it arrives."

"Please tell Dr. Ross instead. He will know what to do with all of it."

"As you request, your majesty." Then Gretchen left.

"We need to get the King to his bed as soon as possible." Dr. Ross ordered.

"I can do that!" Arius announced, and the next thing they knew, they were all in the King's bedchamber. Dr. Ross and James helped the King into his bed. He was very tired and let out a big sigh once he was comfortably in his bed.

"Now, Arius, before I can go to sleep, I must know what has happened in my absence. I think it important for James to know as well so he may stay. Dr. Ross and Justine, thank you for everything you have done for not only me but my kingdom. You may be dismissed to get some much-needed rest."

"You must rest, too. Doctor's orders."

"I will, I promise."

Dr. Ross and Justine left the King's bedchamber as asked.

"Justine, before we go to bed, would you please contact Gretchen to see if the wagon has arrived. I want to make sure that equipment gets here."

"Sure, Dad." There was a period of quiet while Justine communicated with Gretchen and then she offered, "Gretchen said the wagon has come through the gates and will be outside the palace for you to unload in the morning. She will have some guards stand watch over it during the night."

"Tell her thank you. Now I can finally get some rest."

# CHAPTER 32

# NOT THE HOMECOMING
# THE KING WAS EXPECTING

Dr. Ross walked very quietly into the bedroom trying desperately not to wake Stephanie. All he wanted to do was get some sleep. He hadn't slept for two days and wasn't in the mood to talk to anyone right now. He climbed into bed, clothes and all and feel fast asleep. But in the morning...

Stephanie woke up and gradually opened her eyes. There in front of her was her husband. She immediately poked him to make sure he was real and not just her imagination. And then she hit him on the arm.

"Ow, what did you do that for?"

"What are you doing here? Where did you come from? When did you get here? I can't believe it's really you!" Stephanie screamed and then reached for him and gave him a huge hug. "I have really missed you. I have so much to tell you! So much has happened while you were gone." And she hugged him again.

"I missed you, too. I have a lot to tell you as well. I don't know where to begin."

"I have an idea. Let's ring for breakfast and have it here in the room. We can get up and talk while we eat, and with no interruptions, I hope!"

But that idea was short lived. As soon as she said that, there was a knock on the door and Cedric entered the room.

"Dr. Ross, the King would like to see you and Mrs. Ross as soon as possible. Please meet him in the throne room."

"Well, so much for our quiet morning!" Stephanie said disappointed.

"Sorry, Stephanie. Duty calls!"

He waited for her to dress so they could leave. He was already dressed since he hadn't disrobed before he got into bed.

"I think you need to bathe, Drew. You have an odor of dirty laundry about you." Stephanie said as she held her nose.

"Very funny. I'll have you know that Justine washed our clothes at the hospital before we left. However, I have been in them for two days and then slept in them last night. So, maybe you're correct in your assessment of me."

"Okay, stinky, let's go see what the King wants so early in the morning."

Dr. and Mrs. Ross left their bedchamber. Stephanie showed him the way to the throne room since she had gained some knowledge of the palace while her husband was gone. When they arrived, King William was sitting on his throne with Queen Marianne sitting beside him to his left. Standing on his right was Arius.

"Dr. Ross, have you had any conversations with your wife regarding the time period we were gone?"

"No, King William. I went right to sleep last night. I'm sorry to say I didn't even take off my clothes. Why do you ask?"

"I had a long conversation with Arius last night and then with the Queen. Both apprised me of the events that happened while we were gone. They were able to handle the visit from King Henry, but there were complications afterwards."

"King Henry? I wasn't aware that there was another King and Kingdom besides yours. What happened?"

"I am going to let your wife tell you most of it, but what has happened recently is that two of King Henry's soldiers were discovered within our castle walls. Prince John and the Captain of the Guard fought them along with two stable boys. All, but Prince John, were injured in the fight. The Captain is with Dr. Lange and has not regained consciousness yet. I need to address this situation immediately. First and foremost, we need to capture those spies! I need to ask you if necessary, may I travel anywhere by horseback?"

"No, as your doctor, I'm advising you to not leave the palace for a couple more days and to certainly not get on a horse! You're still on antibiotics. We need to make sure you are not in danger of reinfection. Especially since we have left the more sterile environment in the hospital."

"That is not good news. I must think about the consequences facing these soldiers and how to deal with our neighboring kingdom. We cannot endanger the lives of the people who live within these walls nor let those outside find out about the portal. Everyone, please leave me! I need to think!"

"I realize you have asked us to leave, but I would advise you to contemplate your actions from your bedchamber, if possible." Dr. Ross suggested. "I also need to give you your medicine as soon as I can."

"Knowing that you saved my life and are concerned for my welfare, I will overlook your attempt to tell me what I should do right now, and as much as I would rather stay here, I will move to a chair in my bedchamber. You may bring the medicine when you are able. Please knock on my door before you enter. Arius, you will assist me to my room."

Arius left with the King followed by the Queen. Dr. and Mrs. Ross went to their own bedchamber.

"I need to get the medicine for the King. I have it in the backpack in the room. By the way, what happened while we were gone that has made the King so upset."

"I have a lot to tell you but I'll tell you once we return to the bedroom."

When they arrived in the bedchamber, Stephanie asked Drew to be seated because she knew this information would be a lot to take in all at once. Then as she paced back and forth, she explained everything from Luke's ride to King Henry's visit to the spies that were discovered after King Henry left.

"And all that happened because our son chose to go for a ride? Wow! I guess the King has reason to be upset now. What a thing to come home to, especially after just having heart surgery."

"The King had to have surgery?" Stephanie gasped. "I know you said he might need it when you left but I didn't think it was that bad."

"What, you didn't believe me?"

"Well, yes, it's just that I thought after getting him to a hospital that maybe he wouldn't need the surgery. Guess I was wrong."

"Yes, you were."

"Then I bet your trip was rather eventful, too. Please tell me what happened."

So, Drew explained all about the trip through the portal, the ambulance, the trip to the hospital, the surgery, how they had to stay within a mile of Gretchen at all times, about James and Justine..."

"James and Justine?!" She piped in. "What about James and Justine? Do they like each other?"

"Out of everything I just told you, of course you would zero in on James and Justine! Typical," he added.

"Well, I am her mother. What are we going to do about this?"

"Personally, I'm going to do nothing. Just leave them alone. Anyway, we'll be leaving soon, well, as soon as I feel the King is healed. Then it will be over because she won't remember him."

"What do you mean by that?"

"I was told that once a person travels back through the portal to their own time, they lose their memory of their time here unless there is a seeker with them."

"You mean, none of us will remember any of this and we'll just go back to the way things were?"

"Yes, I'm afraid so. Now, I need to get this medicine to the King. We've been talking for quite a long time."

All of a sudden, they heard squealing in the hallway. It was the princesses. They had apparently discovered their father was home and were running to see him. Next, they heard John's voice followed by James all going in the direction of the King's bedroom.

Then their door burst open and Luke and Justine bounded in and gave each of their parents a bear hug.

"Oh, Mom, it's so good to see you," Justine related. "I really missed you."

"Dad, I can't believe you're finally back! So much has happened while you were gone."

"Yes, I know. Your mom told me all about it."

"She did?"

"Apparently you caused quite a stir around here."

"Yes, I did. But I didn't mean to. It just happened."

"Well, I don't know what happened," Justine quipped. "Tell me."

"While you two catch up, I need to deliver this medicine to the King right now."

"Ok," they replied at the same time.

"Why don't the three of us go down for breakfast and you two can tell each other about your adventures. Your dad can join us there," their mom suggested.

"What did you do, Luke?" Justine asked as they walked down the hallway.

"Oh, not much. Just uprooted a whole kingdom, that's all!" Luke and Justine talked all the way to breakfast and spent the next hour trying to outdo each other with their stories.

# CHAPTER 33

## SEARCHED AND FOUND

Dr. Ross arrived at the King's room and knocked on the door as he was told to do. Arius met him at the door. Prince John was there, too.

"I'm here to give you the medicine you need, your majesty and I brought some water. On the way here, I grabbed some equipment from the carriage. One of them will need some electricity if it is available."

"Place the medicine and the water on the table next to me, please," the King motioned toward the table and then continued to stare out the window near him.

"The electricity comes through that little box over there on the wall," Arius informed him.

Dr. Ross was hoping the King's reaction was because he was deep in thought and not because he was experiencing any pain. So, he assumed his role as doctor and began to examine his patient.

"I would like to check you right now, King William, if I may. You're still my patient until you hear otherwise."

"Of course, you may check me. I am feeling just fine. No pain anywhere."

Dr. Ross proceeded to examine the King all over. He even had the electrocardiogram with him so he could check to see if there was any stress on the King's heart. Because this machine was outdated, he had to dig into his memory bank to remember how to operate it. He attached the pads to the King and turned on the machine. He noticed that Arius was watching him very intently. Then Arius started asking questions regarding the machine and how it worked. Dr. Ross explained the procedure to him as he completed each step. He needed to reassure Arius that no harm would come to the King during the exam. Once he was finished, he showed the King and Arius the patterns on the machine and told them they indicated that the King's heart was beating normally and felt the King would be able to resume his usual duties soon.

"That is very good news!" Arius was pleased to learn that the King was healing and the surgery had been successful.

"That is good news, indeed. But now I need to address the issue at hand, the matter of the spies who are still lurking in the castle somewhere."

"Your Majesty, they should not be too hard to find now. I am aware the Captain injured one of them." Arius was confident they would be found soon.

"Yes, that is what I understand as well. Arius, I need you to use your gift of sight and scour the kingdom for any sign of them."

"Yes, your majesty. I attempted this for the Queen when you were gone but they must have been well hidden for I did not see anything. Maybe it will be different this time, especially since one is injured."

Arius closed his eyes and as he started chanting and waving his arms in front of him it was as though he was actually seeing what was happening in the streets within the castle. There were times when he would look down, sideways, and would peer around corners. Then he stopped and stood very still for about a minute. Finally, he opened his eyes and just stared off in the distance.

"Did you see anything that might be of some help?" the King asked.

"I did, your majesty. I noticed some rags near an old house that looked as though they were covered with blood. I think that may be where we will find them."

"Thank you, Arius! And thank you, Captain, for wounding one of them!" the King declared.

"I will gather some soldiers, Father, and go there. Arius, you will need to show us exactly where you saw the rags." Prince John stated as he bowed to his father.

"I hope you are able to capture them. I would definitely like to interrogate them regarding their mission here," the King shared with John. "Bring them to the throne room."

"Yes, Father."

Then John and Arius left.

"Dr. Ross, you will need to walk with me to the Throne Room, please. I am doing much better walking on my own but need someone next to me just in case."

"Yes, your majesty. I'm very pleased with your progress. I'll be happy to walk with you. You have a very strong composition which I think has helped you heal faster."

"I cannot let a little thing like heart surgery stop me from ruling my kingdom!" Then the King got up from his chair and proceeded to walk to the throne room.

Meanwhile, Prince John and Arius had left the palace and moved in the direction of the spot where Arius had seen the rags. Along the way, they recruited some soldiers to assist them. When they arrived in the area, they stopped. John signaled to the soldiers to each move in a different direction in order to approach the house from all angles. The soldiers pulled their swords and walked silently to their assigned spot. Once in place, John signaled to them to move on the house at the same time. He and Arius would go through the front door, with a couple of soldiers entering through the back. The remaining soldiers were to take their place outside the windows in case either soldier tried to escape through them.

John approached the door and kicked it in with his right foot. The door crashed to the floor inside the house. At the same time, the soldiers entered in the same way through the back by kicking in the door. John readied his sword and he and Arius entered cautiously for they didn't know what to expect. They were immediately attacked by the uninjured spy. Arius backed up out of the way as John and the spy began dueling. John was a much better swordsman and the spy decided he wasn't going to win. He ran toward one of the windows and dove through it trying to save himself. He didn't count on the soldiers waiting for him outside and was grabbed without a fight. Prince John heard the scuffle and knew that the spy had been captured. Lying on a bed in the corner was the other one. The wounded soldier looked as though he had lost a lot of blood as there was blood all over the bed around his leg. Prince John put his sword away.

"Arius, you will need to transport this soldier to Dr. Lange as soon as possible. We will bring the other one to the King."

"Yes, Prince John." Arius walked over to the bed, put his hand on the spy and then disappeared.

Prince John walked outside the house and saw the soldiers holding the second spy on the ground with their swords drawn.

"We need to walk this man to the palace. The King wants to have a word with him!" Prince John ordered.

They lifted the spy, tied his hands behind his back and pushed him forward. The soldiers continued to push him along the way to the palace just to assert their authority. Prince John walked along beside them.

The prisoner tried several times to escape but was stopped each time by one of the soldiers who hit him and knocked him to the ground. Then the soldiers yelled at the prisoner to get up and kicked him as he tried to get to his knees. He eventually stood and then was urged forward again. The small group finally arrived at the palace and ushered the prisoner to the throne room where the King was waiting. The soldiers shoved the spy and he fell to his knees in front of the King. Prince John assumed his place beside his father. King William placed his hands on the arms of the throne to brace himself and stood up slowly staring at the spy in front of him.

The King didn't waste any time with his interrogation. "What are you doing in my kingdom? Your King left but yet here you are, still, without the rest of the guard. Why?" the King said forcefully.

"No reason, we just wanted to stay and visit with folk." The soldier moaned without looking up at the King.

"Visit! That is not the reason you stayed here. I think it was to spy on my kingdom! What did you hope to find here?"

The prisoner mumbled something which the King couldn't understand.

"Speak up!" Prince John commanded. "The King cannot hear you. We need an answer right now."

"Nothing, your Kingship, we did not hope to find anything."

"Your fellow soldier is with our physician right now and am assured he will be able to tell us what we want to know when he wakes up. Remove this soldier! Get him out of my sight! Take him to the tower cell and lock him up. Help him remember what he is doing here!" The King ordered his personal guard to remove the soldier which he did.

As soon as the guard had left, the King sank down onto his throne. Dr. Ross started to rush forward and as he did, the remaining palace guards pulled their swords. But Arius stopped him.

Quietly, Arius said to Dr. Ross, "Please remember you are in his Kingdom now. You are not to approach the King without permission."

"Sorry, I won't do it again. I'll remember to ask the King's permission from now on. But that's going to be somewhat difficult for me. I'm still his doctor and he's still my patient."

"Dr. Ross, will you please accompany me back to my bedchambers so that I may rest for a while? I'm afraid this whole incident has made me very tired."

"Yes, your majesty. I would be happy to."

Dr. Ross walked up to the throne and helped the King stand up. They walked side by side to the bed chambers. Prince John and Arius followed them. The King slowly climbed into his bed and lay down on his back with his head propped up.

"It hasn't been very long since your surgery, your majesty. I think you probably overdid it a little. It would be best if you could get some sleep for now." Dr. Ross recommended.

"I think that to be a good idea. I will rest. I would like you to please check in on Dr. Lange to see how the prisoner is doing. John, I would like you to go with him. If the prisoner is awake, try to find out why he and his "friend" remained in my kingdom. And, Dr. Ross, do not be nice about it!" The King requested as he tried to go to sleep.

# CHAPTER 34

## AN UNEXPECTED SURPRISE

Dr. Ross wasn't able to join his family for breakfast because he had to attend to the King. But James and his sisters came down to eat along with their mother. The table buzzed with various conversations and stories that revolved around the adventures each had during the past week. James and Justine had decided before they arrived in Wiltshire to not share everything with Madison and Bethany. There was a lot that they wouldn't understand. They didn't think Queen Marianne would be able to comprehend much of it either, so they would pick and choose what they would tell her.

Madison and Bethany sat wide-eyed as James told them about his experiences. He told them about the elevator because he thought they would understand the idea of something that travels up and down, traveling from floor to floor. They had so many questions that James finally had to ask them to be quiet and leave him alone. Even the Queen had to step in and tell them that they were pestering James with their questions. That's when they started in on Justine. Justine knew she shouldn't get involved in the conversation because she wasn't sure what she could or couldn't share. But of course, she had told Luke and her mom everything since none of it was foreign to them.

"I think we have spent enough time eating our breakfast and need to move on," the Queen announced. "Madison and Bethany, you will please go with your tutor to do your lessons for today. James, you will need to report to the King and discover what your brother is up to."

"Mother, what is the Ross family to do today? May I show them around the kingdom instead of going to find Father? I think John is able to take on anything Father asks."

"None of you are to leave the palace until these two spies are caught," the Queen responded. "There is a reason they are still here and I think it has to do with Luke. You must stay out of sight until they are caught, all of you!"

"Aye, Mother," James acknowledged her request. "We, even Madison and Bethany, right girls, will stay within these walls until the spies are caught. We just need to decide what to do while waiting!"

"The girls are to go with their tutor. They will be busy with lessons today. Madison and Bethany, please go and learn whatever it is you are to study for today." Then the Queen ushered them in the direction of the tutor.

"Do we have to? I think it would be more interesting to remain with everyone else!" Madison said in a hopeful voice.

"Me, too!" Bethany chimed in. "We always miss out on everything."

"The only excitement that you will see today," the Queen stated, "is what will happen if you do not do as you are told!"

"Aye, Mother. We are going," they replied. And Bethany added, "But I am not happy about it." She just wanted everyone to know that she was going under protest.

After the princesses left the room, the Queen requested that Mrs. Ross accompany her to the garden.

"I think we have much to discuss, Stephanie, regarding our husbands and your future here. Please walk with me."

"I think you're right, Queen Marianne. There are some things that need to be decided." Mrs. Ross followed the Queen and they left the Great Hall.

James, Justine, and Luke were the only ones remaining and the three of them sat very quietly for several minutes. Luke finally broke the silence.

"Well, I don't know about you two, but I don't want to just sit here while all of the excitement is going on outside the palace!"

"Luke, the Queen ordered us to stay inside until those soldiers are caught. I think we had better pay attention to that, especially since she is the Queen!" Justine sternly reminded her brother.

"She won't know we're gone. She's out in the garden talking to mom."

"I have a thought," Prince James suggested, "we could stand outside the door to the throne room and listen to the plan and then follow John when he leaves."

"That sounds a lot better than sitting around twiddling our thumbs!" Luke said with excitement.

"Doing what?" Prince James asked.

"Oh, you know twiddling our thumbs, like this," and Luke showed him what he meant. "It means we have nothing to do and are bored."

"With two spies hiding somewhere in the castle, it will not be boring here!" Prince James added. "Come, follow me."

The three of them left the dining room and headed to the throne room. James reminded them that they had to be very quiet so no one would discover their presence.

They walked up to the door and listened very intently to the conversations coming from inside the throne room. When they heard the King order John and Arius to depart, they quickly ran around a corner and stood with their backs to the wall. John and Arius came out of the room and disappeared.

"Where did they go?" Luke asked surprised. "How are we going to follow them now?"

"That, I do not know. Arius used his gift of sight and saw some bloody rags outside a house, but he did not say where the house was." Prince James lamented. "No doubt they went there."

"Won't they need reinforcements? You know, soldiers to go with them? That would mean they have to stop somewhere before they go to the suspected house," Justine surmised.

"You have a point! They will need help. I think we may find them outside near the guard house." James threw in.

"Well, let's go there, then!" Luke echoed.

Just as they opened the door and were about to exit the palace, they heard a voice behind them.

"And where do you think you three are going?" Mrs. Ross had just finished her walk with the Queen and had entered the Main Hall.

"Ah, nowhere." Luke croaked out. "Mom, where did you come from?"

"I just walked in the door from the garden, and I'm guessing it's a good thing I did." Mrs. Ross stated accusingly. "It looks as though you three were about to go out the door."

"No...we just wanted to get some fresh air," Justine said as she started to fan herself. "Don't you think it's a little hot and stuffy in here?"

"Yes, it is. But that's beside the point. I can always tell when you two aren't telling me the truth. Your voices start to crack."

"Craaacck?" Luke responded.

"Yes, like just now. The Queen told you three to remain in the palace and NOT go outside. So, please turn around and march yourselves back inside."

"We are sorry, Mrs. Ross. We just saw John and Arius leave the palace and we were wondering where they were going. That is all." Prince James was hoping his explanation was more believable.

"Well, whatever you were doing, you need to turn around, close the door, and find something else to do."

Prince James closed the door and the three of them sulked off into the Great Hall. Luke ducked behind the door and watched his mom walk up the stairs and disappear.

"She's gone, we can leave now."

"And have both our mothers mad at us? I do not believe that to be a good idea." Prince James declared. "But I have another thought. Another way we can see what is happening. Follow me."

The three went to the back of the palace and James led them up a set of seldom used stairs in one of the towers. They went up several floors before they finally came to another door. This one led to a large balcony that extended across the front of the palace. From there, they had a great view of the kingdom below.

"We may not be able to follow Arius and John, but we can see almost everything from here."

All three strained their eyes looking intently in all directions. Then, off in the distance, they heard clashing, as if metal was striking metal.

"Did you hear that? They may have found the two spies." Luke screeched.

"Shhhh, someone will hear you." James pointed out. "And, aye, it does sound as though John and Arius may have come across something or someone."

"Keep watching. It sounded like the noises came from that direction," and Justine pointed to her right.

They stood very still, hoping to be able to hear or see John and Arius returning to the palace. Then they saw John along with several guards and another person who appeared to have his hands tied.

"There they are!" Luke declared. "I think they got their man!"

They watched until the procession entered the palace. Then they ran to the end of the balcony, bounded down the stairs, and made their way back to the throne room. As they listened outside the door again, they learned that one of the spies had been wounded and was now with Dr. Lange. The other spy was to be taken to the tower and thrown behind bars. Once they had heard what they wanted to hear, the three went back to the Great Hall where Mrs. Ross had supposedly left them. They plopped down in the chairs and Luke got a big grin on his face.

"That was awesome! Thank you, James, for figuring out a way for us to be part of the action."

"It was, as you said, 'awesome', if I do say so!" Prince James affirmed.

The three sat and talked about what they had witnessed for a while. This was all so new to Justine and Luke, and not something James was really used to either.

# CHAPTER 35

## WAITING FOR ANSWERS

Dr. Ross left the King, accompanied by Prince John, to do as he was asked; go to Dr. Lange's office and see how the patient was doing. He knew, as a doctor, he was bound to help those who needed him. He wasn't a soldier. So, on the way, he thought it might be a good idea to seek out one of the palace guards to accompany them.

"Prince John, I think we should ask one of the palace guards to assist you with the interrogation. I don't think I'll be of much help in that area."

"I agree. We will stop by the front door to the palace and ask one of them to come with us."

They explained the assigned task to the guard and ordered him to accompany them. When they arrived at Dr. Lange's office, they found him busy tending to the wounds on the soldier's leg. The soldier wasn't moving so Dr. Ross assumed the patient had been anesthetized. They waited patiently by the door until Dr. Lange had finished. The Captain of the Guard was resting on one of the other beds in the office watching Dr. Lange very intently. Once Dr. Lange had finished, he looked up from his work and noticed Dr. Ross, Prince John, and the guard by the door.

"Dr. Ross, I'm sorry. I didn't hear you come in. I heard you had returned and were able to perform a successful surgery on the King. I'm very glad you're back. I'm assuming you're here to help me with my patients? But, why are Prince John and a palace guard with you?"

"Dr. Lange, sorry to bother you while you're working, but we have been charged by the King to ask the prisoner some questions." Dr. Ross stated as he stepped into the office.

"I don't think he'll be of much use to you at the moment. I had to give him an anesthetic in order to work on his leg. He had a very deep gash which required some cleaning and a lot of stitches. By the way, who is he? No one said anything to me when Arius brought him here. Arius just told me to fix his leg, so I did!"

"He is one of King Henry's soldiers who was left behind when the King left Wiltshire after his visit." Dr. Ross answered. "I think he was left to spy on the good people here. That's what we need to find out. King William sent me to interrogate your patient. But I knew I wasn't up for the task so Prince John and this guard will be doing it instead."

"Now I know what all the hubbub was about earlier. I knew that our soldiers were looking for something, or someone, but I didn't know why. And, I noticed this soldier has a different coat of arms on his armor than the ones from Wiltshire. I couldn't ask the Captain because he is just waking up from his surgery. I had to administer some ether once we returned to the office so that he would rest, and I could do a better cleaning job on his wound."

"I need to report back to the King but I'm going to leave this guard here with you to ensure nothing happens to you. I don't think the Captain will be of much use for a while. I also think it might be a good idea to tie the soldier's hand to the bed so he can't go anywhere."

"That's fine, but I don't think he will be going anywhere on that leg for some time. I'll send word to you when he wakes up."

"Thank you, Dr. Lange." Prince John replied. Then he addressed the guard, "Please remain here and guard the prisoner. If he wakes up, make sure you discover why he is still here in Wiltshire."

"Aye, sir, I will do that. I'll report whatever I learn to the King."

"Thank you. And please, take care not to let the Captain get out of his bed. He has served us well and needs to heal. We leave now but will check on you later."

"Thank you, Prince John, for seeing to my welfare, but I assure you, I won't be getting out of this bed," the Captain affirmed.

Dr. Ross and Prince John left and went to find King William. They didn't find him in his bedchamber and decided to look for him in the Throne Room.

King William had not been able to clear his mind enough so he could rest and had returned to the Throne Room. He was sitting on his throne when Dr. Ross and Prince John walked in. He looked up, acknowledged them, and nodded to the guards that Dr. Ross was allowed to enter.

"Dr. Ross, were either of you able to learn anything from the wounded prisoner?"

"I'm sorry, your majesty, but in order to repair the large cut on the soldier's leg, Dr. Lange gave him some medicine which would make him sleep so he could clean the wound and stitch it up. But John and I asked one of the palace guards to accompany us because I knew I would not do a very good job of interrogating the soldier. The guard remained so he could be there when the soldier wakes up. Also, the Captain is still in the Dr.'s office resting from his wound."

"What to do, what to do?" the King mumbled to himself. "We will just have to wait until he awakes and see what he has to say. Meanwhile, we will need to force the other prisoner to tell us what he knows."

"I'm sorry sir, but what do you mean by "force"? Dr. Ross asked hoping to get a different answer than what he was thinking.

"Force him, do whatever needs to be done to make him tell us."

"That's what I thought you meant. Well, being a doctor, and having sworn an oath to help save lives, I don't think I want to know anymore."

"I understand; you may be dismissed. I will let you know if I need you for anything. John, you may go as well. You made me very proud today."

"Thank you, Father. I was honored to help. I will take my leave now."

"I think I'll go find my family and see what they're up to. But I need you to promise that you will get some rest." Dr. Ross added before he left.

"That I cannot promise, but will do my best,"

Dr. Ross left the throne room. He hadn't seen his family all morning and needed to be with them right now.

"Guards!" the King blurted out. The two immediately moved to stand at attention in front of the king.

"Yes, your majesty."

"I need you to do whatever is necessary to get the information out of the prisoners! One of you go to the tower and assist the guards already there, and the other one must go to be with Dr. Lange. I want to know what they are doing here, who sent them, and what they know. Make sure to find out if they have seen any of the special items we have in our kingdom!"

"Aye, your majesty," the guards answered. Then they did an about face and left the room.

After the guards departed, the King stood up and feeling a little dizzy, paused for a moment. Once he felt pretty stable, he started to walk back and forth in front of the throne as he tried to devise a peaceful manner in which to confront King Henry. He felt he already knew the answers to the questions the guards were ordered to ask the prisoners, but needed proof before he did anything. He knew he might have to travel to address King Henry in person but wasn't sure what Dr. Ross would say to that. Right now, the most important piece of information was whether or not King Henry's soldiers had observed any of the modern conveniences his kingdom enjoyed. If they hadn't, he would be able to return the soldiers to their own kingdom and be done with it. However, if they had seen something, then there would be another decision to make and he didn't want to face that. Now, he just had to wait for answers and waiting was not one of his strengths.

# CHAPTER 36

## A SURPRISE WITHIN THE CASTLE WALLS

"Oh, there you are!" Dr. Ross exclaimed as he rounded the corner of the Main Hall. "I've been looking everywhere for you two. And I see Prince James is with you, too. Excuse me, James, but I would like to know where you two, or possibly three, have been and what you've been up to? Also, Justine, where's your mother?"

"Hi, Dad! And we might ask you the same questions. Where have you been all this time? What have you been up to?" Luke asked. "Why didn't you come to breakfast?"

"I've been …Okay, I'm not here to play 20 questions with you. I would like to know where my family is so we can all finally spend some time together. So, I'll ask again, where is your mother?"

"I think she's in the Great Hall with the Queen getting ready to eat lunch," Justine answered. "They've been together a lot lately, keeping each other company."

"Thank you for your help, Justine. I'll go find her and I expect you two to remain here until I get back."

"We will, won't we, Luke?"

"Yes, we certainly will."

Dr. Ross left the hall in the direction of the Great Hall to see if he could locate his wife.

"Wow, I wonder what part Dad played in all of this?" Luke pondered. "I know you all just returned and the King is still under Dad's care. So, I'm assuming the King can't do much without Dad being around. I wonder if he helped with the capture of the soldiers?"

"He was probably with my father if he was needed. However, Father would not have included him in the plan and capture of those two soldiers." Prince James asserted. "That would have been for my father to decide."

"Why are you asking, Luke?" Justine questioned.

"Oh, nothing really. I just think that there may be more to our dad than meets the eye. He knows a lot more than he's saying. Why was he gone all morning?"

"Luke, your dad and my dad have been through a lot together and have formed a bond because of it. But my father is still the King and has to do his duty to protect our kingdom no matter how strong the bond between them. Your father has no experience with a sword, and so my father would not put him in a position to have to defend himself."

"Boy, you're right there! When would my father or any of us have need to use a sword? Now a scalpel he could handle." Luke threw out.

"What is a scalpel?" Prince James asked.

"It's a small knife used to cut a person's body open so a doctor can operate. But boy are they sharp!" Luke commented.

"Your father used that during surgery on my father?" Prince James asked looking concerned.

"Yes, he did. But it was necessary. It's a very small knife." Justine explained seeing the look on Prince James' face. "All surgeons use them."

"I'm tired of being stuck in this palace. Can't we do something? Maybe go outside and walk around?" Luke inquired. "I want to see more of the kingdom before we have to start out for home."

"Dad told us to stay here until he gets back with mom. Maybe he has something planned for all of us to do. He said he wanted to do something as a family."

"Yes, he did. Okay, I guess I'll have to wait, then." And Luke sat back in his chair looking disgusted.

Then they heard footsteps running down the stairs. It was Madison and Bethany followed by Prince John.

"Well, this is exciting, the whole family is here!" Luke said sarcastically. "And I suppose the princesses want us to do something with them."

"Just ignore him," Justine stated. "He is just mad because he doesn't get to do what he wants."

"I found these two girls sulking upstairs and thought they needed a break from their tutor. So, I asked them if they wanted to do something a little more exciting, and of course they said yes. They wanted you to be part of it so we came to find you three." Prince John announced.

"We are tired of being inside and want to have an adventure," Madison stated.

"Aye, and we have come to ask you if you want to go with us." Bethany asked.

"I suppose that depends on the adventure you are proposing," Prince James replied.

"Well, you found us. So now, what's this exciting plan?" Luke asked.

"We thought we could ride bicycles around the village." Madison suggested. "That is not something we get to do very much. We thought Mother and Father would let us since we have guests and the danger of the spies in the kingdom is past. But, from the way you are speaking, I think you want to stay here and not go with us."

"I think your idea is wonderful!" Justine insisted.

"Actually, I think that is a great idea!" Luke announced. "I wanted to go for a walking tour of the village, and this would be the same thing only on bikes. I'm in."

"Very good! Glad you like our idea, Luke. I love to ride the bicycles," Bethany shared. "Sometimes we are allowed to ride them outside the castle walls, but not very often. Horses are scared of them. Maybe we could have a picnic, too."

"Come girls, let us go find the bicycles and get some lunch to take with us." Prince James shouted. "This will be a wonderful adventure!"

"Right!" they said simultaneously.

Then they all walked toward the back of the palace where the bicycles were stored. Justine stopped, looked around and then said, "Our dad told us to stay here and wait for him. We can't leave yet."

"You may write him a note to let him know where you have gone. If he knows, he will not worry." Prince John suggested.

"Okay, I hope he won't be mad that we've gone off without him."

Prince John found some paper in one of the drawers in a large desk and a writing tool and gave it to Justine. Then she wrote her parents a note telling them where they had gone with the royal family.

They stopped in the kitchen to get some food for the picnic. The kitchen maids insisted they do all the work preparing the food since it wasn't proper for a member of the royal family to work in the kitchen. Justine remained there until the lunch was ready and the others went to the back room in the palace to ready the bikes.

By the time Justine joined them, the bikes were all set up and ready to go.

"I can't believe you actually have bicycles here In Wiltshire. How long have you had them?" Justine asked.

"The bicycles have been part of our kingdom ever since Dr. Lange came. He brought one with him when he first visited our kingdom. We liked them so much that when he returned to get his medical equipment, we asked him to bring enough for all of us and a few extra for the people in the village to enjoy. Gretchen had a hard time getting them all through the portal."

"I bet she did!" Justine affirmed. "That gave her good practice for all the medical equipment we brought back with us." Then they all laughed trying to picture Gretchen carrying so many bicycles.

"Let us go so we can return before dark." Then Prince John got on the first bike and started off on the path outside the palace. "Come on, we have a very large kingdom to cover and also have a picnic."

The rest of the group hopped on their bikes and followed Prince John down the path. Right behind the palace was the back wall of the castle. It loomed up over them like a protective shield against anything that might threaten the people. They followed the path along the back wall for a while, past the end of the palace, to the corner where the back wall ended and became the west wall. From here, they could see the houses and shops of the villagers stretched out in front of them since this part of the castle was high on the hill on which the castle was built. It became very clear at that moment that the castle walls protected many people. They could see the palace guards standing watch along the tops of the walls and in the turrets at the front gate. They could also see the tower on the east wall where one of the prisoners had been taken.

"We will begin our tour here. On the way, there is a wonderful place to stop for our picnic." Prince James declared.

"My stomach is telling me that I am hungry!" Bethany announced. "I hope we stop soon."

"Bethany, the tour has not yet begun and you already want to stop!" James declared.

"It is my stomach that is the problem."

"Well, you will just have to wait, little one." Prince John replied.

"I am not little any more. I am ten now."

"You will always be my little sister, and there is nothing you can do about it. Now, let us get started. Follow me." And Prince John set off in the lead with everyone following single file.

Prince John and Prince James would point out places of interest as they rode. Luke and Justine became very aware of the standard of living in the 1500's, the material from which the houses were made, the living conditions, the way the food was prepared and cooked, the clothes they wore, the street markets and the items bought and sold there, what they used for money, and even about the farmland that was outside the walls. They were both fascinated by it all and asked lots of questions.

They came across a beautiful little hill in the outer courtyard that had a dirt path leading to the top where a grand oak tree stood. There were flowers lining the path all the way to the top. At the top was a large boulder just below the tree.

"This is where I thought we could have our picnic," Prince James announced. "This is a very famous hill and an important part our kingdom's history. That big oak tree is said to be over a thousand years old."

"Did your history have anything to do with that boulder at the base of the tree?" Justine inquired.

"Aye, it did. Why do you ask?" Prince James looked at Justine somewhat baffled.

"Aye, why?" Prince John threw in.

"Remember when we were at Stonehenge and we were waiting for the ambulance to arrive and..."

"Am-bu-lance?" Madison repeated very slowly. "What is that?"

"I'll tell you in a minute, Madison. Anyway, my dad needed to know your last name so he could register your father at the hospital."

This time Bethany interrupted, "Hospital, what is that?"

"Girls, please let her finish," James asked of his sisters. "Go ahead, Justine, please finish what you were saying."

"Okay, you stated that your last name is Pendragon."

"Pendragon? As in King Arthur's Pendragon?" Luke burst out.

"Yes, Luke. The very same. James, Dad asked you if you're related to King Arthur and you said yes. According to the legend that is told in our history books, there was a famous sword called Excalibur and whoever pulled it from the stone was the rightful king. King Arthur was the one who pulled it from the stone, or boulder as it may be, and he was declared king."

"He built Camelot, created the famous round table of knights and fought many battles." Luke added. "He also had an infamous sorcerer called Merlin, was always battling Mordred, and there was also the Lady of the Lake...!"

"You two know a lot about King Arthur." Prince James said surprised.

"Oh, yes! He was a very famous king! There are books, movies, songs, poems, all written about him. I can't believe you are related to him! That is so cool!" Luke was definitely flabbergasted by this new information.

"Our family is a direct descendent of King Arthur and Arius is a descendent of Merlin." Prince John affirmed.

"Then I'm confused," Luke began, "Why is your kingdom called Wiltshire and not Camelot?"

"Camelot was the castle of King Arthur. It was a very important part of his story. He created it! After his death, his descendants let the legend of Camelot die with King Arthur and changed the name of the castle to Wiltshire. It is the same place but with a different name. That way the name of Camelot is synonymous with King Arthur and no one else." Prince John relayed.

"Oh, wow! So, this is really the famous Camelot! I can't believe we are actually here where King Arthur lived." Luke exclaimed!

"That's why I asked the question about the boulder up there. I thought that might be the famous stone that held the sword." Justine shared. "Can we go up and see it? Can we touch it?"

"I thought we would picnic under the tree. So yes, we can go up there and yes, you can touch the boulder. But it is forbidden to climb on it." Prince James took Justine's hand and they started up the path together.

"James, you and Justine? What happened while you two were in Oxford?" Luke asked as he started up the path behind them.

Then James realized he and Justine were holding hands and they immediately let go and acted as if nothing had happened.

Madison and Bethany joined in with, "James and Justine, James and Justine!"

"I think that is enough out of you two," Prince James quipped. "Let us just go enjoy the picnic."

# CHAPTER 37

## THE FIGHT

The picnic quickly became one of the highlights of the tour. They sat under the tree for about an hour talking about the Pendragon family history, the kingdom of Wiltshire, about Luke and Justine's home, what it was like in Indiana, about the schools they attended, anything that popped into their heads. And because the princesses asked, Justine and Luke tried to explain what an ambulance was as well as a hospital. James was the only one who could grasp the concept of both since he had actually experienced them.

Justine and Luke made sure they laid their hands on the boulder and tried to look for the split in the rock where the sword might have been. But erosion had washed any trace of it away after so many years.

"James, may I talk to you for a minute?" Prince John asked.

"Aye. I will be back in a moment." James then followed John to the side of the hill away from the others.

"I need to ask to something, and I did not want the others to hear, especially Justine. What is going on between you two."

"I like her. There is nothing wrong with that is there?"

"Yes, there is, little brother."

"Do not call me that! I am of age and can make my own decisions. I can decide who I like and who I do not like."

"Have you forgotten they will not be staying here and need to return to their own time? As soon as Father is well, they will be leaving, never to return. They will not remember their time here once they walk back through the portal."

"I do not care about all that. She is here now! We grew very close when we traveled to her time and took Father to the hospital. I do not want to lose her."

"They are not like us! We are to be matched to someone from Wiltshire. We are wed by the time we are twenty. Dr. Lange told me that people in their time do not marry so young. They are still learning at something called a college until they are twenty and two years!" As James turned away and started to leave, John grabbed his arm and turned him back. Looking at him he said, "She is not going to want to stay here and marry you. You are not facing what is real!"

"I want to, I am trying to! But she has become too important!" James proclaimed.

"What are you two talking about?" They both turned around and Justine was standing there. "I don't know if you realize it or not but you two are yelling at each other. Your sisters are worried about you, and so are Luke and me."

"How long have you been standing there?" Prince James asked.

"Not long. I just walked over here. Why?"

"No reason. We were discussing something private that we did not want anyone to hear."

"Can you please come back and join the rest of us so we can finish our food?"

"We will be right there."

"Great, I'll go let your sisters know that you're just talking." Justine turned, walked back to the picnic spot and sat down next to Madison and Bethany. "Your brothers told me that they needed to have a private conversation and that's why they walked way over there. They want you to know they are just talking even though it was loud."

Then, all of a sudden, they heard grunting noises and the sound of someone falling to the ground.

"Look, Justine, they are fighting!" Bethany screamed.

All four of them jumped up and ran over to where Prince John and Prince James were fighting.

"Do not tell me what to do!" Prince James yelled and then he hit John on the chin with his fist. Prince John fell backwards and landed flat on his back. Then Prince James stood over him and held him down with his foot. Prince John grabbed his brother's foot and twisted it so James lost his balance and fell next to him.

"Luke, do something! They're going to hurt each other!" Justine said as she grabbed Luke's arm to push him toward the fighting brothers. "You know karate, or judo or something. Use it!"

"What do you want me to do? I'm only one person!" Luke declared.

So, Luke walked over as the two boys were getting to their feet and asked them to stop fighting. He pointed out that Madison and Bethany had started crying. But that didn't work, so Luke took his stance and began throwing his arms and legs in their direction using various Karate moves he had learned in the dojo. His foot struck Prince John in the chest and he went flying backwards. Then Luke hit Prince James in the side with his left hand and then turned and hit him in the face with his right foot. Then he stood his ground and looked at both boys waiting for them to move again.

"I asked you very politely to stop fighting and you didn't so I needed to ask you with more force. I'm sorry if I hurt either one of you. I can keep going if I need to," Luke stated forcefully.

Both of the brothers were now trying to catch their breath and Prince James put his right hand up in the stop position toward Luke while he stood there bent over with his left hand on his thigh.

Out of breath Prince James conceded, "No, that was enough. Where did you learn to fight like that?"

"And Prince John, what about you?" Luke asked. Then Prince John stood up and Luke looked straight at him ready to continue fighting if need be.

"I think I also have had enough, thank you."

Justine ran over to Prince James to see if he was all right and helped him straighten up.

"Your face is bleeding!" Justine started to blot his mouth with her hand.

"I am fine." Prince James said as he brushed her hand away which surprised her.

Madison and Bethany ran over and both put their arms around Prince John and gave him a big hug.

"Ow, be careful. My middle is a little sore." And he hugged them back.

"Are you okay? My brother can throw some pretty mean punches. I'm glad he was able to get you two to stop. We were worried about you both. What could you have been talking about that made you fight like that?"

"You." Prince John replied. "We were fighting about you."

"Me?" Justine said with a look of surprise on her face. Then she couldn't help but smile because that meant that James must like her, a lot, and that made her happy. But getting serious again she said, "Why were you fighting about me?" She couldn't wait to hear the reason.

"Do not worry about it now," James replied. "We can talk about it later."

Justine looked disappointed but knew she would have to wait to talk to James about this. She went to grab James' hand but he pulled it away and put it at his side.

"We should gather all the picnic things and head back to the palace. Our parents are probably worried about us." Prince John suggested.

They went back to the tree, gathered all the picnic items, and walked back down the path to their bicycles without saying a word. At the bottom of the hill, Justine stopped her brother for a moment.

"I want to thank you for stepping in like that. I'm glad you were able to get them to stop fighting."

"I wasn't sure if I could do anything, but I guess my Karate training finally paid off!"

Justine was still not sure what had happened and why James was acting so strangely. His behavior toward her had changed and she wasn't sure why.

No one talked as they rode back to the palace. They went along the back wall, the way they had come and placed the bicycles in the back room where they had found them. Then they all made their way back into the palace. As they were walking into the kitchen, Justine grabbed James by the arm.

"James, is everything all right? You seem different all of a sudden." Justine asked hoping they could talk.

"We need to talk later after everything has calmed down."

"Okay." James could hear the disappointment in her voice.

They followed the others into the Main Hall and there they were met by their parents. Even the King was waiting for them.

"Where have you been?' King William demanded. "You left the palace without permission and with this issue regarding the prisoners unresolved."

"We are truly sorry, Father. It will not happen again." Prince John affirmed.

"We went on a picnic, Father. John and James took us on a tour of the kingdom to show Justine and Luke." Madison added.

"Aye, Father, we had a wonderful time! We went to the hill to show them the old oak tree and the boulder!" Bethany said with a big smile. "We were having so much fun until John and James started fighting and that ruined everything."

"John and James started fighting?" Queen Marianne inquired. "Yes, you did! I can see that now that I look at you two. What made you so mad that you had to fight about it?"

"John said they were fighting about Justine," Bethany teased.

"Fighting about Justine?" Mrs. Ross threw in. "Does this have anything to do with the trip to Oxford?"

"Now, Stephanie, let's not go there right now." Dr. Ross suggested.

"The trip to Oxford, while my husband was recovering from his surgery?" Queen Marianne asked. Her voice started to sound agitated because she realized that she wasn't told everything that had happened while the four of them were gone. "So, what have you not told me about that trip? Did something happen between James and Justine?"

"Queen Marianne, they were together a lot waiting for the King to heal. It was very innocent; nothing happened." Dr. Ross assured her. "Justine showed him around and introduced him to the 21$^{st}$ century."

"James did admit to me, as we were preparing to return home, that he liked her." King William announced. "But they are just friends, I hope. John and James, please follow me to the throne room. I think we need to find out what this was all about." Then the three of them left.

"Justine, I would like to talk to you. Let's go to your room where we can have some privacy." Mrs. Ross insisted. "Drew, why don't you come, too. And Luke, I suppose you should join us as well."

Dr. Ross and Justine looked at one another and Justine shrugged her shoulders. "Yes, mother." Justine lamented. And the family walked up the stairs to Justine's bedroom.

Queen Marianne, Madison, and Bethany were left in the hall.

Queen Marianne asked, "Is there anything you want to share with me regarding this whole incident?"

"No, mother. We only know that James seems to really like Justine and maybe John teased him about it." Madison pondered.

"They were really fighting, and then Luke stepped in and really let them have it!" Bethany declared as she illustrated some of his moves. "He was fighting in a way I have never seen before. I would like to learn how to fight like that!"

"Thank you, girls. That will be quite enough out of you, Bethany. I think you two need to go to your rooms until dinner, which will be soon since you returned from your outing so late."

"Do we have to?" Bethany pleaded.

"Yes, now go." Queen Marianne scolded.

Queen Marianne stood in the middle of the hallway all by herself. Inside, she wanted to scream because she knew the outcome was going to be very difficult for James. But she was the Queen and needed to contain her emotions, especially in public. For now, she had to wait.

# CHAPTER 38

## A RESOLUTION

The King sat down on his throne trying to gather his thoughts. He had become aware back in Oxford that James liked Justine, but wasn't prepared for the direction this relationship seemed to be heading. He would have to dismiss Dr. Ross so he and his family could return to their own lives. Also, with no strangers in the kingdom, it would be safe for the time being. It was easier to keep "things" hidden rather than people. He needed to begin this conversation and it would start with his two sons who were standing before him.

"Please explain to me the circumstances surrounding this fight you two had on our sacred hill no less!" the King began.

Both boys started talking at once and the King couldn't understand a thing they were saying. He put his hand up to stop the boys from talking and they became silent.

"John, you begin, please. I want the truth, nothing made up!"

"Aye, Father. It started when we were getting ready to walk up the path to the tree and James took Justine's hand."

"It just happened! I just did it without thinking."

"James, you need to remain quiet. You will have your turn when John is done."

"Aye, Father."

"Please continue, John."

"As I was saying, James took her hand and the girls began to tease him about it. Once we all started eating, things calmed down. We had some good conversations and found out a lot about each other. Then I told James I needed to talk to him and we walked over to the side of the hill so no one could hear us. I told him he should not get close to Justine because her family would be moving back to her time. I told him what I had learned from Dr. Lange about their world and how their lives are very different from ours. Father, I also told him he cannot expect her to stay here. Then he got mad and we started fighting."

"Thank you, John, for telling your side. Now, James, you may talk."

"Father, John was trying to tell me what to do. I did not like it, so I hit him and that started the fight."

"That is all you have to say for yourself? There has to be more to the story than that!"

"There is, Father, but I don't think you are going to like what I have to say."

"I think I know what it is you are going to say, but say it anyway."

"I think I might be in love with her. When John confronted me and said she would be leaving and I would never see her again, I got angry and scared all at the same time. She means too much to me."

"That is what I thought. John, you may leave. I would like to talk to James by himself."

"I will leave you two alone." So, John left the throne room.

"This attraction you have to Justine has to end."

"But, Father!"

"As King, I can order you to end this for the good of the kingdom. I can give you all kinds of reasons why this will not work, but I will not do that. I am going to talk to you as a Father and not a King. Son, I know what it is to have a first love. I once thought I loved a young princess from another kingdom. She looked very much like Justine. I was your age when I met her. When I learned that I was being promised to someone else, for the good of the kingdom, I was devastated. I sat around for the next several weeks with a broken heart. Then I met the young lady who I was promised to, your mother, and that princess became a distant memory. I fell in love with your mother the moment I met her and we have been in love ever since."

"I was not aware that you loved someone before our mother."

"This is not a well-known part of my life. It would please me greatly if that information does not leave this room."

"I will not tell anyone. I understand why you told me this, but it does not make this any easier."

"I know that, James, but you are going to have to find a way to let her go. Talk to her about it and help her understand as well."

"I will, but how will I know when that "right time" will be?"

"You will know. So, for now, enjoy her company, but do not do anything that might strengthen your bond to each other. You may leave and please know that the Ross family will most likely be leaving in the next couple of days."

"The next couple of days? That is too soon, Father!"

"The sooner they leave the quicker you will be able to move on. Would you please tell Gretchen that I need to see her? And send Arius in, too."

Then James left the room. His mind understood what his father was telling him to do, but his heart had other ideas. He had to be by himself for a while to think things through and figure out the next steps.

# CHAPTER 39

## THE PRISONER WAKES UP

As James was leaving the throne room, he passed Arius in the hallway.

"I was just on my way to get you. My father would like to speak to you. But it seems you already know that." James said.

"Your father and I have an unbreakable bond and we can sense the thoughts of the other. But right now, I have some important information to deliver to him."

"It seems you are found, then. That is one person off my list."

James left to locate Gretchen to let her know that the king had requested her presence. He found her near the front door. After she left, he went to his room so he could be alone.

"Arius, do you have news for me?" the King asked as he stood up.

"Aye, your majesty. The prisoner being cared for by Dr. Lange has awakened. He has been questioned and I can relay his answers to you."

"Well, do not delay then. Tell me what he had to say." King William demanded.

"It took some doing, and a lot of coaxing, but he told us that he and his 'friend' were told to stay behind by King Henry. He said King Henry was sure something was amiss in our kingdom and he wanted to know what that was. They were to look for anything that was out of the ordinary. He did ask about the strange sight on wheels he saw a boy riding. I am sorry, your majesty, that was all we could get out of him before he passed out."

"This is not good news! I was hoping to be able to deliver them back to King Henry with nothing to report."

"Your majesty, I have a suggestion."

"Aye, what is it?"

"I can make them forget having seen anything with one of my spells or make them forget they were even here if that is your wish."

"Arius, that is a wonderful idea! I have not had a clear head since the surgery and I forgot you have that power. I think it best they not remember anything concerning the bicycle. King Henry would definitely suspect something however, if they do not even remember being here. One more thing, can you remove the memory of their capture and let them think that they escaped on their own?" King William was formulating a story that he hoped would be believable. "But something had to have happened to them since one soldier is in the tower, probably hurt, and the other was wounded..."

"Aye, may I suggest something?" Arius inquired,

"I would be most appreciative if you would," the King stated.

"To begin, we were unaware that two of King Henry's soldiers had decided to stay behind and chanced upon them in a pub. Not knowing why they were still in the kingdom, a fight broke out and one of the soldiers was badly wounded. The other one panicked and cut his leg when he jumped out the window to escape. Being a kind and caring people, we decided to see to their wounds, and they were attended to by the physician to the King. Then, as soon as they were able to ride, we sent the two of them off on their merry way never to come back again."

"Excellent, and you can put all of that into their heads so they don't remember what actually happened here?"

"Aye, your majesty, I can."

"Wonderful!" The King stated. Then he turned to the guards standing by the door. "Guards, you need to tell the soldiers in the tower to immediately stop their interrogation of the prisoner. We have all the information we need. Then, let Dr. Lange know if the prisoner needs any medical attention, I mean, someone to tend to his wounds."

"Medical attention?" Arius questioned. "Must be a term you acquired while on your journey to the other side of the portal."

"Sorry, I need to be careful now. It is important I not use unfamiliar terms around the people in our kingdom or outside of our kingdom!" King William proclaimed.

"Agreed! I will go and ready our prisoners for their departure. I think Dr. Lange said the soldier in his care should be ready to travel in a day or two. After I am done, both soldiers will have a different story to tell than the one they actually experienced."

"It has been a very long day. I am tired and need to rest for a while. Before you use your magic on the soldiers, would you please walk me to my bedchambers? I hope I can finally get some sleep. Also, tell Dr. Ross I need to speak with him first thing in the morning? There are some things we need to discuss." Then the King got up from his throne, took a deep breath and he and Arius walked down the hall to his bedchamber. The situation with the prisoners had been resolved and he felt greatly relieved. Arius did not want to leave the King, so he sat in a chair until the King eventually fell asleep.

# CHAPTER 40

## THE DECISION IS MADE

The two families, minus James, gathered together the next morning in the Great Hall for breakfast. The princesses couldn't stop talking about the events of the previous day and hardly anyone else got a word in during the meal.

"Where is James?" Bethany asked. "He must be hungry, too. Why is he not here with us?"

"He had a long talk with Father last night in the throne room." Prince John confirmed. "I am not sure when they finished so he may still be sleeping. He will probably be down soon."

"What were they talking about?" Justine questioned. She hoped she hadn't been the topic of conversation. She didn't want James to get into trouble because of her. She really liked him and missed him when he wasn't around.

"Do not worry about him, Justine. I am sure he will be here soon." Queen Marianne assured her.

Then Arius appeared in the Great Hall and banged his staff on the floor to gain everyone's attention.

"Dr. Ross, King William asked me to summon you this morning. He asked that you join him in the Throne Room. He has some things he needs to discuss with you. When I left him just now, he was much more like his old self. I think he finally may have actually slept through the night."

"Thank you, Arius. I'll go right away." Dr. Ross excused himself from the table and left very quickly. He wasn't sure if he was needed as the King's doctor or not. As he was leaving the hall, James appeared at the doorway. Justine looked up, saw him and smiled but James glanced away and looked at his mother.

"Mother, I cannot eat right now for I am not very hungry. If you will please excuse me."

"Please eat something, if not now, later."

"I will." He couldn't look at Justine right now. He knew he would have to talk to her about her families' departure and he wasn't ready for that. He turned very quickly and left.

Justine's face just dropped. She couldn't understand why James was avoiding her. Ever since the picnic he had been very cool toward her. Was it something she said or did? Was he mad at her? Did his father say something to him that made him not want to be with her? She was so upset that she just couldn't stay at the table.

"Mom, I need to be excused, please." Justine said as she started to tear up.

"Sure, honey. Are you okay?" her mother asked very concerned.

"Yes, I just can't sit here. I'll be in my room." Then Justine got up from the table, walked quickly to the doorway, and then ran up the stairs down the hall to her room.

"What is wrong with Justine?" Bethany muttered. "She does not look very happy."

"If you will excuse me as well." Mrs. Ross lamented. "I think I need to go talk to my daughter."

"Yes, please. Attend to your daughter. I think she may be in need of advice." Queen Marianne insisted.

"The Ross family may be leaving soon," Prince John informed them. "I think Father is well enough for them to return home."

"Leave? I do not want them to leave!" Madison asserted. "Since they have been here, life around this palace is far from boring!"

"We have been having so much fun with them." Bethany affirmed.

"Leave? What makes you think that, Prince John?" Luke asked. "Do you want us to leave? Is that why you just had to throw that into the breakfast conversation?"

Then Madison and Bethany started sobbing because they were not prepared to hear this news.

"Now look what you have done, John!" Queen Marianne scolded her son. "You could have waited until a more opportune time to announce this."

"I am sorry, Mother but I am only stating the truth."

Then Madison and Bethany got up and ran out of the room still crying.

"Well, I know when I'm not wanted," Luke stated. So, he got up and left the room as well.

"John, you and I will have a conversation about this later. But right now, I need to attend to my own daughters. I hope you are happy. You just cleared the hall."

Queen Marianne left the hall leaving John alone at the table. He looked around and muttered to himself, "I was only telling the truth. I do not know why everyone got so upset." He shrugged his shoulders and proceeded to eat his breakfast.

Meanwhile, Dr. Ross had arrived at the Throne Room per the King's request. He was stopped by the guards at the door until permission to enter was granted by the King. When the King saw him, he motioned for him to come in. Dr. Ross noticed that Arius and Gretchen were also there.

"Dr. Ross. Glad you were able to come. Sorry if I interrupted your breakfast."

"I wasn't hungry anyway," Dr. Ross answered. "Are you feeling all right, your majesty? Arius said you needed to see me right away. But he did mention something about you getting a good night's sleep last night."

"I am doing as well as can be expected given the events that transpired yesterday. I think I have faced a whole week's worth of problems."

"I'm sorry to hear that, your majesty. May I get you anything?"

"No, thank you. That is not why I summoned you here. We need to talk about you and your family returning home soon."

"Returning home? But you still need to be cared for by a doctor at least for another week or two."

"You have been with us for almost two weeks and I think there are probably many who are in need of you in your own time. And you forget, Dr. Lange is here permanently and you have provided him with much needed medicine and equipment. I think he will be able to take care of me once you leave."

"Yes, that is true. Then I will need to relay some specific instructions on your daily care and on the chance you relapse, which is highly unlikely at this point."

"Things have calmed down now here. It seems we will be able to send the two prisoners back to their own kingdom very soon. We now know why they were here and what they saw. Arius can expel those memories so they will have nothing to report to their King when they arrive home. I have also had a conversation with my son regarding your daughter. It seems they have become very close during their time together and my son cares deeply for her. It will not be easy for him to say goodbye to her. The problem is that he will have his memories of her but once your family goes through the portal your family will have no memory of us."

"Your majesty, I had no idea you were faced with all of that these past two days. I can understand why you've been so tired." Dr. Ross acknowledged. "As to my daughter, I knew that they had become good friends but wasn't aware that it had gone this far."

"You must remember, that our traditions are very different than yours. Our young men are often married by the time they are twenty. Prince John will need to marry very soon and James will be next in line."

"You're thinking marriage! Justine is still in high school and no where near ready to get married!" Dr. Ross declared.

"High school? Well, never mind what that is right now. The point is that your family will need to leave before this relationship goes any further. Your Justine will not want to remain here in Wiltshire and I cannot have my son consumed by her to the point he cannot marry another young lady from our kingdom."

"I understand, sir. I need a clarification on something, though. You stated that once we go through the portal, we won't remember anything."

"That is correct."

"Will we remember the visit to Oxford from the first time we went through the portal? We didn't lose our memories then."

"The portal will erase all memories you have of anything here or connected to here unless there is a seeker with you. So, the entire week we were in Oxford should have been something you would not remember. But Gretchen was with us."

"But won't the people in Oxford remember us being there and the surgery?... And you just said would have been. What does that mean?"

"What you ask is true. However, Gretchen was able to erase the fact that James and I were there and changed the name of your patient right before we departed. She couldn't erase the whole trip, which I would have preferred, since you had given your speech from that hospital. I did not tell you this when we left. That will be a memory for you and Justine but not for Stephanie and Luke. So, for them, Gretchen said she will plant the memory of being in a hotel in Oxford. The rest, you will need to figure out after you go back through the portal.

"So much happened there! I'm glad I will remember most of it. At least Stephanie and Luke will have something to remember, too. I suppose I need to inform my family we will be going home. When do you propose we leave?"

"The sooner the better I'm afraid. Gretchen will be your guide just as she was the last time you went through the portal. But this time, she will be returning without you. We will be sending the prisoners on their way tomorrow so that means you may leave as well."

"I'm glad to know that this has all been settled and that we will be able to return to London soon. You're looking very tired, King William. May I help you to your room so you can rest?"

"Yes, I would welcome the assistance. Thank you."

The King rose from his throne and Dr. Ross walked with him to his bedchamber. Then he left to find his wife. Arius and Gretchen departed as well to prepare for the Ross family to go through the portal.

# CHAPTER 41

# A DIFFICULT CONVERSATION

"I don't know what's wrong," Justine questioned through her sobs. "He wouldn't even look at me when he came into the Great Hall."

"I'm sure you didn't do anything wrong. There must be something else affecting his behavior. You just need to talk to him," Mrs. Ross suggested as she tried to comfort her daughter.

Just then the door opened and in walked Dr. Ross and Luke.' "We're glad we found you. We didn't know..."

"Please sit down and don't say anything." Mrs. Ross said. "I'm sorry Justine, please finish what you were saying."

"He's been avoiding me ever since our picnic yesterday." Then she stopped and tried to relive in her mind the events that had transpired since they stopped for the picnic. "Maybe it was the teasing from his sisters, and my brother, and now he's embarrassed to be with me. No, that can't be it! We sat together under the tree while we ate. It must be something that John said to him and that's why they were fighting."

"I bet it was just a disagreement between brothers. That happens a lot."

"I need to find out what was said between them so I can get back to the way we were." Justine wiped her eyes, and took a deep breath. "Thank you, Mom. I think I know what I have to do."

"I'm not sure how much help I've been, but you're welcome."

Justine got up, straightened her clothes, checked her face because she didn't want to look like she had been crying, and set off to find James.

Turning to address her husband and Luke, "I'm very glad you two didn't say anything just now. Thank you for just sitting there and listening."

"I didn't know what to say, especially since I know how the King feels about all of this." Dr. Ross said. He knew his daughter was upset and didn't want to make matters worse.

"Same for me, too, Mom. For once, I thought it best if I kept my mouth shut." Luke added.

"Well, I don't know how all of this is going to end for them, but I hope they can work it out. And, since we appear to be leaving in the morning, we should gather what little we have together so we're ready."

Justine didn't find James in his bedchamber so she decided to try the first floor ending up in the Great Hall. But he wasn't there either. She was beginning to lose hope when Cedric walked into the hall.

"Cedric, have you seen Prince James by any chance?" Justine inquired.

"Aye, miss. He went outside toward the garden and has not returned."

"Thank you, Cedric!" And she gave him a hug which startled him because no one in the royal family ever hugged him.

She took off toward the garden and went outside. She looked all around to see if she could see him. But no James. All she saw was a myriad of colorful flowers spread out before her. The garden was rather large and had several paths winding through it. If she was going to find James, she needed to pick one and start looking. As she started down one of the paths, she caught a glimpse in the distance of what looked like a gazebo surrounded by bright pink flowering bushes. She moved closer and noticed someone was sitting in it. She took off running because she knew it was James. She was right! Sitting on a bench in the middle was James. She slowed down because she didn't want to startle him or possibly scare him away. She got to the gazebo and saw James bent over with his head in his hands, like he was thinking. She walked quietly up the stairs to where he was sitting. He looked up, saw her and immediately stood up.

"Justine! What are you doing here?"

"I came to find you. You have been avoiding me ever since yesterday and I don't know why. So, here I am, asking."

"I am sorry Justine. Aye, I have been avoiding you because I could not face you knowing we needed to talk. But now that you are here..."

"Talk? Have I done or said something that hurt you in any way?"

"Truly, no. You could never do anything wrong, Justine. To me, you are perfect!"

"Oh, wow! I wish I were, perfect that is. Then what's wrong?"

"You remember the picnic and Bethany teased me about grabbing your hand."

"Yes, of course I do."

"Well, John wanted to talk to me about it. He didn't approve. It made me angry so I hit him and we had a fight."

"About me?"

"About you. I told him how I felt, feel about you and you know what happened."

"How you feel about me? How *do* you feel about me?"

Then James moved closer to her and grabbed her right hand. "I care about you, a lot. You have become the most important person in my life. I love being with you. You are funny, smart, kind, and beautiful and I think I am in love with you. That is why John and I were fighting. He blamed me for letting this get this far."

"Wait, go back to the part where you think you love me. Really?" she blushed. "So is this the discussion you were dreading because I don't think this is difficult at all! In fact, I feel the same way!"

"You do? That is... going to make this even harder!"

Justine grabbed his other hand, "Make what harder?"

Then James said quietly, "The fact that you will be leaving soon."

"Leaving?" And she dropped his hands. "Who said anything about leaving?"

"My Father, the King. He said that he is going to dismiss your father from his obligation to care for him. Dr. Lange is here and can now assume that duty."

"That's not fair!" Justine said as she started to cry.

Then James pulled her to him and hugged her as hard as he could. They just stood there, entwined, for several minutes while she cried into his shoulder. She looked up at him with tears glistening in her eyes and he kissed her.

"We have always known, in the back of our minds, that your family would return to your own time to live out your lives there. But now, things are different! You have found your way into my heart and there is nothing I can do about it."

"I could stay here, with you!"

"No, you have a life in another country, another time. And you must return to that. I must stay here and follow the path I was on before I met you. This is why I have not wanted to see or talk to you. I did not want to face what is real, wanting this go on forever."

"Oh, James. What can we do?"

"One thing that will help *you* when you return is that once you go through the portal, and Gretchen leaves you, you won't remember any of this. Life will go on as if you were never here and I never existed."

"But you do exist, even if it's in the 16$^{th}$ century! I can't forget you, I won't. I will remember you." And she reached up and kissed him.

Then James took a step backwards and placed the arms that had been holding him to her sides.

"What about you?" she asked quietly. "You won't be going through the portal, will you?"

"No."

"So that means I won't remember you, but you'll remember me?"

"Aye."

They both stood silently for a minute and then James took her hand again.

"That will be the hard part. Trying to forget you for I know you will always be with me." He looked down, cleared his throat, and took a deep breath. When he straightened up he said, "I think we need to return to the palace."

The two of them silently walked hand in hand back through the garden to the palace. When they entered the door, the rest of the world came alive as the voices of the palace began to surround them. They looked at each other for a moment embracing each other in their gaze. Then Justine pulled her hand away, turned and walked into the palace. James could hear Bethany greeting Justine in another room. He heard Bethany begin to cry as she told Justine how much she would be missed. His heart was breaking as he faced the idea of life without her. He heard the voices fade as they moved farther into the palace. He was already missing her and she hadn't even left yet.

# CHAPTER 42

## LEAVING WILTSHIRE

Dr. Ross spent part of that afternoon explaining to Dr. Lange all the medical needs regarding the King. Once he had finished with Dr. Lange, he went to help the family prepare for the trip home. But there really wasn't much to do since they could only return with the clothes and any personal belongings they brought with them. They couldn't take anything or have anything that reminded them of Wiltshire for the kingdom would be a long-forgotten memory once they were home.

As Justine was looking around for her things, she remembered the necklace that she had been given in London. Could she take it home with her and possibly stay connected to Wiltshire? Would she still be connected to Gretchen even back home in Indiana? Would she even recognize the necklace for what it is once she goes through the portal? She didn't have any answers to all of these questions, but she decided to keep it just the same. So, she put it around her neck and hid it under her shirt like she had ever since it was given to her in London.

There was a knock on her door.

"Come in."

"Hey, sis. Just wanted to let you know that I'm here for you if you need me."

"Thank you, Luke. I appreciate that more than you know. Did you realize that once we pass through the portal and Gretchen leaves us that we won't have any memory of this place? It will be like we were never here."

"Really, why? I don't want to forget all of this. This was the best part of our vacation! What if we want to come back sometime? Will we be able to? It would be fantastic to be able to come back and visit, to see everyone again."

"Yes, it would. But we can't so I don't want to think about it right now.

"Oh, sorry. I forgot about James. I guess you will forget about him too, after we leave."

"I guess so," Justine muttered.

"Well, I was supposed to come get you so we can all meet in the Main Hall. Are you ready?"

"Ready for what? I thought we weren't leaving until tomorrow morning."

"Well, I guess it was decided it would be better if we left now."

"Now, that's not fair! I wanted to have just a little more time."

"Hey, Justine, I'm really sorry about you and James. But what good would it do if we stay longer? You're going to forget about him anyway."

"I know, but we're still here and he is still here and here is where I want to be."

"We need to get downstairs now. Everyone is waiting. So again, are you ready?"

"No, but I guess that doesn't matter right now. So, I'm as ready as I'll ever be."

Justine looked around the room for one last time trying very hard to burn the memory of it and Wiltshire into her mind. She was hoping, if she did, she would remember *something* when she returned home, even if it was just a small thing. Then she followed Luke down the hallway, down the main staircase to the hall. Everyone was waiting there, from both families as well as Dr. Lange, Arius and Gretchen.

"There you are, you two. I thought we were going to have to send the guard after you!" Dr. Ross joked.

"Do you have everything?" Mrs. Ross asked.

"Mom, we didn't come with very much in the first place! Just the clothes on our backs! And besides, we aren't allowed to take anything with us anyway." Luke replied.

"Yes, Mom, I have everything," Justine said with a sigh. She looked up to reply to her mother and as she did, she caught James looking at her. She couldn't help but smile back and then looked away.

"King William, I think my family is ready to begin the journey home." Dr. Ross announced.

"Very well. I want to thank you for all you have done for me and my family, Dr. Ross," the King stated with deep gratitude in his voice. "You saved my life and for that I will be eternally grateful. Now I am here with my family which, at one time, I thought would not be possible. I also want to thank your family for befriending mine. That has been a blessing for them. You will be missed."

"I can't go without saying that this was certainly an unexpected detour during our vacation, but one I wouldn't have missed for the world. The only downfall of this whole thing is that we will return home and not remember any of this, which is truly a shame." Dr. Ross responded.

"I am sorry for that, but we need to protect our kingdom from those who might do us harm from the outside. It has served us well these past one hundred fifty years and I hope for another one hundred fifty. Children, say your goodbyes to the Ross family."

Bethany and Madison ran over to Justine and hugged her for a long time. Then they backed up a little and started to cry.

"I feel like I am saying goodbye to my sister." Madison shared through her tears.

"Me, too!" Bethany added. "Maybe you can come back and visit us sometime?"

"I would like that." Justine answered.

Then the two of them walked over to Luke to say goodbye.

"We want to hug you, but Father said we need to act like little ladies and just curtsy." And then Bethany and Madison both curtsied in front of Luke. "You are so adorable, Luke! More than any boy in the whole kingdom!" Bethany announced.

"That is enough young ladies. Now move over here by me." Queen Marianne coaxed the girls to her side.

Prince John was next. He walked over and put his hand out and he and Luke shook hands. "I really am glad we had the chance to meet, Luke. Your visit was certainly one of excitement and adventure."

"Yes, I guess I did bring a little excitement to your kingdom!" Luke affirmed.

"And Justine, you have taught my brother about many things from your time which I hope someday we will find useful for the people in our kingdom."

Then he moved to Dr. Ross. "I want to thank you most of all for saving the life of my father. This kingdom cannot bear to lose him. He has been and will continue to be a just and caring King. He still has a lot to teach me before I will be able to take his place." Then John and he shook hands and John bowed to show his respect.

James was last to say his goodbyes to the Ross family. He started with Dr. Ross and also thanked him for saving his father's life. Next, he moved on to Mrs.

Ross and then Luke. Then he faced Justine. The words didn't seem to come. He didn't know what to say to her that he hadn't said in the garden.

And then finally, "I want you to know how much your friendship has meant to me these past two weeks. I will miss you most of all. I think you will always be with me no matter what." Then he took her hand and placed it over his heart. "In here."

Justine tried very hard to be brave and not cry. But when she looked up at him, tears filled her eyes and she immediately looked away to try to compose herself. He held her hand for another moment, then let it go and walked to where his family was standing. Queen Marianne put her arm around him because she knew he was saying goodbye to his first love.

"Arius will transport you to the portal and then Gretchen will take you through it. We hope the future is kind to your family and wish you good health and prosperity." The King stated.

"You need to stand in a circle and hold hands so we can all travel together." Arius instructed.

Then Arius mumbled something and the group vanished from the palace hall and immediately reappeared in front of the portal.

"This is where I must take my leave of you," Arius informed them. "Gretchen will see you safely through the portal and return you to your own time."

No sooner had they all said their goodbyes to Arius then he disappeared.

"Justine and Dr. Ross, you have already gone through this portal three times so you should know how this goes by now. Mrs. Ross and Luke, I need you to go behind Dr. Ross and then Justine will follow. I will be the last one through to make sure there are no problems. I have added a spell to the portal so that when you come out on the other side you will be invisible. That is a precaution in case there are people at Stonehenge. You will remember everything when you arrive on the other side for a short while. Then, once I release you, you will resume your life as it was before you came to Wiltshire. I cannot return you to the tour that brought you to Stonehenge because that spell was already used when Dr. Ross went through with the King. That is the only week you will recall and remember you have been gone for two weeks. Your phones will be working again and you will be able to call for transportation to Oxford and then on to London."

"We'll be invisible? I could do anything I want and no one will see me!" Luke announced.

"All right, we need to get started. Dr. Ross, will you please begin?" Gretchen motioned for the family to get in line behind him.

Dr. Ross entered followed by Luke and Mrs. Ross. Justine hesitated before she entered and turned around to face Gretchen.

"Gretchen, you just said we would remember the week in Oxford. That means that Dad and I will remember James and King William, right?

"I am sorry, Justine, but you will not. You will remember the week, the hospital, and the surgery but the King and Prince James will be replaced by different people in your minds." Gretchen informed her.

"That's not fair! I want to remember! Look, I still have my necklace! Will that make a difference in what I remember?"

"I'm afraid not..."

"Well, no matter what, I'm going to wear it home! It's mine now and no one can take it away from me! And, since I still have it, will I be able to communicate with you and maybe be able to return someday?"

"I do not know if the powers will work so far away from here nor do I think it has the power to help you remember.

You might get faint glimpses of memories as if you were dreaming but that may be all. Someday, if you find yourself in England again, the power of the necklace may return. But that has never been tested in all these years. No one has ever returned, except for Dr. Lange. Maybe the necklace loses the magic after a while."

"I don't care what you think you know about the necklace. It's never been tested so I guess I'll be the guinea pig and I hope you're wrong about it."

"What is a guinea pig? Never mind. Right now, we need to go through the portal before the magic wears off."

Justine entered the portal followed by Gretchen. Once on the other side Gretchen gathered them together. They could see each other but they were invisible to anyone else. Gretchen looked around and didn't see anyone visiting the site. So, she waved her hands as she said a chant and they became visible.

"I want you to know that it has been an honor to serve this family. I am glad I was sent to locate you and bring you safely to Wiltshire. Going to Oxford and observing the surgery on the King was an experience I will never forget. But now, I must leave you and let you get on with your life here in your time."

"Thank you, Gretchen, for all your help in Oxford. Without your help, we would never have made it to the hospital on time." Dr. Ross stated with appreciation.

"From now on, you will be on your own." Gretchen said another spell to release them and she became invisible to them. She waited a short while to make sure the spell had worked. As she turned to leave, she noticed Justine was looking at her as if she could still see her. Justine waved and muttered, "Good bye." Then it dawned on Gretchen, Justine was wearing the necklace. She waved back and disappeared into the portal.

"Who are you waving to, Justine?" her mother asked.

"Oh, I thought I saw someone but it was my imagination."

# CHAPTER 43

## BACK HOME AGAIN

"Hey Mom and Dad, there's no one here! I can't believe it! I think the tour left without us! What are we going to do now?" Luke inquired.

"Well, I'm not sure," Dr. Ross answered as he looked around. "Let me check my phone. That's funny. My phone shows a date that is about two weeks after we took the tour. Maybe it's broken?"

"Let me check mine," Luke replied. "Oh, wow! My phone shows the same date as yours. What happened to the last two weeks and why are we still standing here? Why did the tour leave us stranded?"

"I've heard of people getting amnesia, but a whole family?" Mrs. Ross threw out.

"I think we have been on a trip somewhere, but right now I can't remember where. It's all so fuzzy. I can't seem to pull it into focus yet." Justine said with a puzzled look on her face.

"A trip? How come you can remember that and we can't?" Luke challenged.

"However, what I do remember was for one week of the two we've been gone. I remember someone being sick and Dad had to operate at a hospital in Oxford?"

"Wow, you have some imagination!" Luke announced.

"Let her alone, Luke. She obviously believes she remembers something about the past two weeks.

It's certainly a much better explanation than I can come up with." Mrs. Ross put her arm around Justine. "Well, whatever happened, we have been gone for about two weeks. You know what, now that you mentioned Oxford, that seems to ring a bell."

"Maybe we were abducted by aliens. That could have happened especially at a place like this."

"No, I don't think we were abducted by aliens! Your sister's explanation makes more sense than yours does!" Dr. Ross stated, "And for some reason, I remember someone needing surgery, too... and in Oxford. We can figure this out later, but right now, we need to find some transportation so we can get back to London."

"Oh, my goodness! I totally forgot about the hotel! They probably think we got lost or something." Mrs. Ross said frantically. "We need to devise a story to tell them when we get back that is believable, one we all agree to."

"I'm going to call a place I know in Oxford to see if we can get a taxi or something to come pick us up. Wait a minute! Why is this phone number listed in my contacts on my phone? I think I'm beginning to remember more now, about Oxford. It's still somewhat fuzzy. Anyway, since it will take about an hour for the taxi to get here, we can decide what we are going to tell people about where we've been for the past two weeks."

Dr. Ross called the service on his phone he had used before and asked them to send a driver to Stonehenge. The family found a shady spot to sit while they waited. They all started talking at once trying to offer their own explanations as to the families' "disappearance". Finally, Dr. Ross said he would decide what the story would be and that everyone had to be on the same page if their story was to be believable.

However, he wasn't sure why, but as they continued to talk about different scenarios, he continued to have flashes in his memory of being in Oxford early in their vacation and that he had operated on someone. He also remembered Justine being with him in the hospital. But Stephanie and Luke were not part of this memory. He assumed Justine had the same memory as he did since she mentioned a surgery earlier. He decided to use that as their reason for being gone. He worked out the details to the story based on this emerging memory.

"Here's the story we're going to tell people when they ask where we have been for two weeks. Our family decided we wanted to visit Oxford instead of returning with the tour group. Then, on the way to Oxford, we came across a man who was walking along the side of the road. He seemed to be having trouble walking and was holding his chest. Naturally, being a doctor, I couldn't just pass this poor man by without offering to help. We stopped and asked him if he needed a ride somewhere. We found out his car had broken down and he was walking to get help. We took him to the hospital in Oxford. On the way there, I realized he was having trouble with his heart. So, I had to do surgery on him to repair a valve in his heart. He had to remain in the hospital for the next week. I had to stay at the hospital and Justine stayed with me. Stephanie and Luke, you stayed in a nearby hotel. His family was so grateful for the kindness we showed to this man that they invited all of us to their house in the countryside. There, I continued to attend to the needs of this man for the next week. And, that is what happened during the last two weeks! Okay, everyone got the story straight? Any questions?" Dr. Ross wondered.

"No, I think that about covers it." Luke admitted. "But how come Justine got to stay with you at the hospital and Mom and I stayed in a hotel? Oh wow, you know what? I don't think that was just a story you made up! I think that actually happened!"

"I think you're right, Luke! That story really happened. It isn't just one I made up! And why are we just now able to remember it. Oh, and by the way, why are we back at Stonehenge if this took place in Oxford? There is something very strange going on here and I'm not sure what at the moment." Dr. Ross was totally confused by all of this and needed more time to hash this out in his head.

"Dad, I remember this, too. We were in Oxford and you operated on a man. You and I stayed in the hospital for some reason. And, you delivered your speech for the symposium from the hospital! And I watched!" Justine recalled.

"And I do remember being in a hotel in Oxford while you remained at the hospital," Mrs. Ross added. "So why are we here at Stonehenge? That part is certainly a mystery!"

"Well, I guess my made-up story isn't so made up after all! But the answer to why we are here still eludes me!" Dr. Ross said. "Oh, good. I think I see the driver coming. Now let's get back to London!"

In the car on the way to Oxford, Justine leaned over to her father, "You remembered that, too? I do wonder why you and I chose to stay in the hospital and Mom and Luke stayed in a hotel?"

"I don't know Justine. We may never figure this all out. At least we're together and that's all that matters."

The family finally arrived in Oxford and then traveled on to the hotel in London. They walked in the front door up to the main desk.

The clerk at the desk had just dropped something on the floor and reached down to pick it up. When he straightened up, he saw Dr. Ross and his family. His eyes opened really wide in a look of shock.

"Dr. Ross? Where did you come from? You've been gone for over two weeks! We had no idea where you were!"

"Well, we're back right now and wondering if our room is still available."

"Oh, sir, we didn't know where you were. You never came back after your tour. Your tour guide returned your backpacks that you left on the bus and stated that one of the members of the tour had become very ill and you and your daughter went with him to the hospital in Oxford. But he didn't see your wife and your son when that happened. They searched the area around Stonehenge for them but finally gave up and came back to London. Once you had been gone for two weeks, and your reservation here had ended, we gathered all your belongings and put them in storage. We didn't know what to do!"

"That's okay. We understand. We didn't have any cell service where we were and couldn't contact anyone. Do you have a room we could stay in for now? Our airline reservations are not for another week."

"Absolutely, sir! Let me see what we have available. Oh, yes, I think you'll like this room. You'll be staying in the presidential suite on us."

"That is very generous of you! Thank you!" Dr. Ross acknowledged.

"Here are your keys. Please enjoy. I will see that your belongings are brought to your room. Let me know when you will be checking out."

The Ross family enjoyed staying in the Presidential Suite for the remainder of the week. They decided it was best to stay in London and not venture out of the city for the rest of the vacation. During the rest of their stay, they revisited some of the same sights they had seen earlier in the trip that Mrs. Ross had missed.

During one of the tours of London, Mrs. Ross noticed that the necklace was missing from Justine's neck. "Justine, why aren't you wearing your necklace? You told me you were never going to take it off because you were afraid you would lose it."

"I'll put it back on when we leave. And you're right, Mom, I don't want to lose it. I feel very attached to it, like it's part of me. But last time we were in London, I kept seeing things and I thought it would be better to not wear it while we're here."

When their three weeks were up, they packed all their belongings in their luggage and placed the bags by the door to be picked up by the hotel service. Justine made sure she had her necklace on before she put her bags by the door. She walked back into the room and went over to admire the necklace in the mirror. While she stood there, she noticed it glow like it did when they were in London at the beginning of the trip. But this time, it didn't scare her. Now, it just made her feel safe.

The family checked out of the hotel and took a limo to the airport.

"I'm glad I don't have to haul Justine's luggage around this time!" Luke declared.

"You will need to help once we get back home," Justine assured him.

"Now, you two, don't start. Let's have a nice, peaceful ride home, okay!" Mrs. Ross requested.

They checked in at the ticket counter and walked to their gate to wait for the plane. At the gate, they found some seats close to each other and sat down. Dr. and Mrs. Ross decided they wanted to get some coffee and left Justine and Luke to watch the carry-on luggage. Justine decided to check her phone to see if there were any messages. She had cleaned it out when they were in London which took a while since she hadn't looked at it for over two weeks. When she looked up, she saw a figure dressed in black standing on the other side of the walkway.

"Luke, do you see that person over there dressed in black?"

"Where?"

"Across the walkway, right over there!"

"I don't see anything."

"You're kidding! Right over there!"

"Nope, sorry. You must be seeing things again!"

"Oh, good grief! I really did see a figure in black when we were in London. I wonder why that person is staring at us?" But this time, the fear seemed to disappear as she continued to watch the figure across from her, and she felt like she knew this person.

Their mom and dad returned with their coffee and sat down.

"Mom and Dad, I am not seeing things, but remember in London when I saw the figure in black? Well, it's back and I'm not afraid of it this time."

"Justine, I'm sure you saw something when we were in London the rest of us couldn't see. But to have it appear now, at the airport? I can't believe it would be watching us again." Mrs. Ross was trying to rationalize what her daughter thought she saw.

"Hey, maybe that black figure had something to do with our memory loss and why we found ourselves at Stonehenge?" Luke threw in. "Spooky isn't it?"

Her mother opened her purse and took out the journal she had purchased in Oxford.

"Mom, you still have that? Have you written anything in it so far?"

"Yes, as a matter of fact, I have."

"May I see it? Maybe it has some answers to the mystery of Stonehenge?"

Justine started to read what her mom had recorded throughout the trip. She read about the tour to Stonehenge and then...

"What is this about a place called Wiltshire, Mom?" Then right before her eyes, all the words on that page and those following it disappeared. "Mom, the words in your journal just disappeared! How did that happen?"

"I don't know. Let me see it."

And sure enough, the words that had been written about the time spent in Wiltshire just disappeared.

"That is very strange, kinda like this whole trip, right Mom! And why did you write about Wiltshire?" Then, she looked across at the figure in black and felt a strange attachment to it and Wiltshire for some reason.

"That's very true, so very true! And why *did* I write about Wiltshire? I have no clue."

There was an announcement that the flight was loading so they all got ready to board for their return home. As they were boarding, Justine kept looking back over her shoulder to see if the figure in black was still there and it was. As she handed her ticket to the person at the gate, she heard a voice say, "Goodbye". She turned around and the black figure was gone. She followed her family on to the plane for the trip home.

Once in her seat, she closed her eyes and visions of people she didn't know started to appear in her mind. She also dreamt about them whenever she slept on the plane. One in particular was always in her thoughts. He was a very cute young man whose presence made her feel all warm inside. Whenever she envisioned his face, she felt as if she knew him and he was someone special in her life, but she didn't know why. One thing she did know was that she didn't want to forget his face or that feeling.

# CHAPTER 44

## HOPE FOR THE FUTURE!

"Gretchen, is she safe? Does the necklace still work?"

"Yes, Prince James, she is safe and the necklace still works just as you had hoped."

"Thank you, Gretchen."

# ABOUT THE AUTHOR

As a young girl, reading was not one of my favorite past times. I would much rather sit and watch a movie than read a book. But this changed when I became a teacher. I loved to read the books my students were reading and looked forward to the conversations we would have about the characters. I also realized how much I enjoyed teaching my students to write. Because of this, I decided that one day I would write my own book but didn't realize how long it would take me to put those words on paper. Now that I have retired, I have finally accomplished the goal I set for myself. Unexpected Detour is the result and I hope you enjoy reading it.

Pam Knowles resides in Carmel, Indiana, USA. She is married and the proud parent of three children and Nana to six grandchildren.